NO ONE IS INNOCENT

A Novel By Sam Lobley

First published by Dog Ear Publishing
4011 Vincennes Rd
Indianapolis, IN 46268
www.dogearpublishing.net

ISBN: 978-1-4575-3910-7

This book is printed on acid-free paper.

This book is a work of fiction. Places, events, and situations in this book are purely fictional and any resemblance to actual persons, living or dead, is coincidental.

Printed in the United States of America

For the Portledge Class of 2015

Prologue

Detective Pearson sauntered into the Houston Police Department as he did every day. The excitement of the big case has now come and gone. It was all a matter of paperwork and he could feel his mood sliding into a slight depression. Avoiding eye contact with others in the hallway, he quickened his pace until he arrived at his small shared office.

The kid wasn't in yet, but Pearson didn't care. *Probably just running late.* He sat in his faux leather office chair and looked at the newspaper articles and copies of evidence that decorated the overused cork board. The desk in front of him supported a pile of papers that would easily take a whole day to organize. The prized possession lay on top—the entire course of events, as told by a secretary-turned-amateur-sleuth.

In truth, Pearson felt defeated. He did not solve the case, nor did his partner, the kid, who went by the nickname "Suds." He knew all too well that they chased their tails and never found any reliable leads. But the girl, the person he ignored, overlooked… she asked questions. She knew what happened before he and Suds could even make guesses. She was out there discovering information while they just sat around thinking the case would never be solved.

The hefty detective rolled his chair over to the small, plastic coffee machine and pressed the power button. It roared into motion like a car on the brink of breaking down. He prayed, as he did every day, that it could produce just one more cup of coffee. Luckily, the warm, brown liquid once again filled the cheap styrofoam container.

That's one crappy cup of coffee, he thought. He had to wipe the remnants of a first sip off of his thick, bushy mustache. He knew it was graying, but he wouldn't dye it like his wife said to. *I'm not scared of aging*, he would tell her. *I'm embracing it*. She would roll her eyes.

He wheeled back and the door opened. The kid was out of breath and his clothes were disorderly, hanging off his body. He tossed the sunglasses off his face and sat down in his chair.

"How's it going, boss?" he said aimlessly. Pearson gave his usual nod.

Suds looked at the pile of papers and sighed. The case was over, so why did they still have to deal with it all?

"This case isn't fun anymore, is it?" Suds said to himself.

"Nope," Pearson said. His throat was a little sore and his voice sounded garbled. He tried to take a sip before his lungs gave out a cough. *Yep, I'm definitely getting older*, he thought.

"We said today was the day. We're going to take down some of these newspapers. Listen, I know we're still trying to cling to hope, but we're not going to find her. I'm afraid she's gone." Suds proceeded to take down the headlines, one by one. "BILLIONAIRE MURDERED" was printed on nearly all of them and Pearson winced. He knew all too well the girl was gone and he couldn't quite digest it. The search wasn't officially called off yet, but it had already been a month. The old detective felt the store-bought blueberry muffin in his stomach.

"There, doesn't it look better?" Suds said. Pearson didn't look. "I'll go throw these away." His partner hugged the scattered newspapers in his arms and fled the room.

It was hot from the building's strong heating system and Pearson was already breaking a sweat. Memories of the case flashed in his mind as he stared at the papers on his desk. A picture of the cold dead body. The witness reports. The revelations and lies that continued to pop up even days after he was called to the scene.

His heart raced as he flipped through the pages of the girl's report. She knew it all. The arrests were made a couple of weeks ago. He was all too aware as he read her final words. They weren't typed like the rest of them. They were an after thought, scribbled in beautiful, neat handwriting. "No one is innocent." He let out of a breath of air and tossed the packet of papers—her fantastic final report—in the trash.

Chapter One

It was January, and an unforgettable chill permeated Clara's bones. Surely, it was not that cold, nothing frozen or anything like that, but she wasn't accustomed to the briskness. It was a time when the city of Houston was experiencing an actual winter, and everyone was panicked. Just a few days ago, Clara had to purchase a heavy coat that could withstand the low temperatures. A colossal waste of money. The low temperatures would soon be over, and the weather would return to its usual comfortability. Nevertheless, she was cold.

As the clock ticked to seven, she was just arriving at the office. It was early and she was tired, but there was too much to be done. The keys fumbled around in her fingers for a moment before falling to the ground. The palms of her hands were unusually sweaty, despite the temperature. Her knees let out a groan when she retrieved the keyring—a painful reminder that she was in need of exercise. When she eventually clasped the keys and inserted the correct one, the lock turned and she leapt inside. The waiting room offered no warmth and was dark, but did not smell like the usual overpowering and sickening scent of "calming candles," as they were called.

When the lights came on, Clara quickly made a mental checklist. Turn on the heat, the TV, place the magazines, arrange the desk, etc. And then into the doctor's office to prepare for the day. She would normally throw her purse on the desk, often causing it to tumble off, before starting up the coffee machine, but this time she carefully placed it down and proceeded to empty the necessary contents.

After arranging the waiting room, she entered the doctor's workroom (the *therapy* room) and gasped. She wasn't loud enough to wake him. Lying on the old leather couch, with a pathetic blanket draped over his body, was Dr. Weihen himself. In a fit of outrage, Clara flipped the lights on and pushed his limbs and shook his frame until his eyes opened. Pretending to feel sorry for waking him up, she whispered over him, "Victor, what are you doing?"

It took him a few long seconds to react. His face began to flush and the color of his skin became a strawberry-red. Embarrassment? No, anger. Clara braced for the worst. He rubbed the crap from his eyes and said, "Clara, the real question is why on earth are you here so early?"

She longed for the new year to change his unbelievable rudeness, but her wishes were in vain. His eyebrows dramatically converged at the top of his nose in that ridiculous look of contempt he wore every day of his life. His messy, gray hair only contributed to the hideousness. Victor Weihen was one of those people that would make a caricature artist's job very easy. He nearly always looked upset and the features that would normally be exaggerated and blown up in a sketch were already on his face, and certainly couldn't be missed. The unsettling part of his appearance was that he was only thirty seven years old, but could almost pass for seventy.

Clara said, "Victor—"

"Dr. Weihen. We're at the office. Call me Dr. Weihen."

"Dr. Weihen," Clara gritted her teeth, "Since we just had a few weeks' break, I figured I should make sure the office was prepared for the day." She panicked. The doctor wasn't supposed to show up until nine. There went the time she had for herself. Now, she knew Victor would start giving her minuscule jobs to do that only interfered with getting through the arduous eight hours of work. She continued, "What I didn't expect, doctor, is to see you here. Especially in such unordinary circumstances. May I venture to guess why you are sleeping on the couch in your own office?"

"No, that information is not for you to know." He started folding the blanket.

"Well, then I suggest you go into the bathroom and wash your face. You have several patients today." He left the room with nothing to say, the creaks echoing as his feet pounded on the weak floorboards. Clara knew exactly why he was sleeping there: his marriage was nearing its extinction. Victor's wife, Janet, occasionally visited him at the office and it was always a bad sign when she did. Without fail, she would storm through the front door, a frown plastered to her face, before screaming at him in the therapy room. One day, it would be about paying a bill and another day, it would be about how she wasn't seeing him enough. It escalated when he had forgotten their anniversary. Clara heard everything. The walls were so thin.

Things got heated again before the holiday when she confronted him about her father. He supposedly developed dementia and Victor would not pay for the man to be sent to a nursing home. Victor was a bastard— he certainly made enough money. Clara had seen his paychecks. He just didn't want to do it. It was awkward for Clara at the time, but she couldn't just leave the office. She had to hear the excruciating sounds of Janet yelling, then sobbing and Weihen sighing, then punching his desk. Or was it the wall? They didn't make up, though. Clara heard a slap and Janet rushed out, slamming the door so hard the building shook. It wasn't good at all. And now Victor was kicked out.

As the sound of the sink gushing resonated through the waiting room, Clara decided it was time to arrange the office for the day. Only a few things needed to be done. She set the doctor's notepad on his desk, placed the medicines in their ideal position in the cupboard, and lit those terrible candles. She fluffed the cushions on the couch and stored the blanket in the drawer underneath the doctor's desk. As she was ready to return to the waiting room, there was just one more thing. The small surveillance camera that had been placed in the doctor's office a while back still remained, and there was really no use for it anymore. It was flimsy to begin with, and started to malfunction slightly before the holiday. She removed it before it would become a nuisance, or before the doctor noticed it.

When she marched through the waiting room to her receptionist's desk in the corner, there was just half an hour until the first patient would arrive. Clara took advantage that Victor was still in the bathroom to apply makeup, wipe off her glasses, and situate the desk. For a long time, she stared at the single pen that sat atop a neat stack of papers at the top of the hutch. It was not the only pen at the desk, but the only one that patients used to sign forms with after their appointments. It was a sad little pen that lost its cap long ago, yet it was a workhorse that Clara presumed would have outlived the universe. She picked it up and tested it to find that it was dried out, and then dabbed the tip in liquid before replacing it to its proper spot. It really was an immortal pen. She admired its resilience.

The young secretary awoke from her pen-staring trance when she heard the noise of the bathroom door open. Victor stepped out with his hair combed and his face shaved. His situation was worse than she thought. He had clearly been sleeping at the office long enough to have bothered to bring a comb and razor. Who knows what else he had with him? Yet, she still refused to produce any sympathy from her heart. He gave a cold look and promenaded to his office, shutting the door just slightly harder than one normally would. It was then that Clara clicked on the television, only to hear the awful noises of a reality show about poor people swapping houses with rich people. Utter trash, but patients seemed to enjoy it. She pressed the mute button and turned on captions. A whole day having to listen to it would not suit her well.

When the first patient, a man by the name of Leiman Turner, walked through the door, Clara fidgeted in her seat. Eight months. Every day. The same boring thing. The first patient through the door, mumbling a "good morning" before sitting and staring blankly at the wall. Would she ever get away from it? Would she *want* to?

Turner was a bit different, this time, because he walked over to the desk looking vaguely disappointed. He asked, "Is the coffee machine working?"

Clara did not quite understand what he meant, but then looked over at the coffee dispenser and saw that she had never turned it on. It was rather a rare event because she drank coffee like it was a religion. She must not have been in the mood that day. Apologizing, she turned it on and eventually handed him the hot drink in one of those boring styrofoam cups that she never liked. She preferred paper.

The doctor opened the door to his office and invited Turner in. They were in there for a good part of the hour, and Clara was uncertain of what they were doing. Usually she eavesdropped with the little camera, but that was not an option anymore. She knew very little about the patients' conditions because Victor tended to keep things "confidential." She was forbidden to peruse the files she worked so hard to keep neat. Turner might have been there for depression; he just looked so damn passive all the time. She couldn't assume anything, though, because she really had no working knowledge of psychiatry. She was offered the job because of her intelligence, diligence, and in all probability, her favorable looks. She accepted because of the pay. And there was really nowhere else to go.

The next patient, who arrived just ten minutes before Victor's conclusion with Turner, was Mitch Greenway. To describe the arrogance that this man possessed would be a life long endeavor, which would only cease when the world ran out of paper. He was an extremely wealthy businessman. As any affluent Texan, he made his money in the oil industry. Well, *he* didn't make his money, but his father and grandfather did. He just sat on the money his family had already amassed and benefited from the profits of the company, the Greenway Oil Corporation. He had a son, Miles, who was about twenty-five and seemed to be more promising than his father.

Greenway saw Dr. Weihen to supposedly relieve stress and tension, according to Mitch himself. It is a secret that he visited a psychiatrist, known only to Victor, Clara, a handful of other patients, and his family (Miles and his wife, Linda). Mitch suffered from paranoia— Clara knew that much—and believed if it were to be publicly known that he sought mental help, investors and such would assume the company was unstable. It was a ridiculous idea, but then again, Mitch Greenway was never too sharp.

He came in his usual three-piece suit, dark sunglasses, and tailored camelhair peacoat. He never made eye contact with anyone, even Clara, given the secrecy of his visits. He retreated to the corner of the waiting room, soon to be sucked into a magazine. Usually he read *Forbes*, but this time he took some long document out of his briefcase and began reading it over. Clara was interested to know what it was but the door to the office opened and Turner walked out. He was carrying a sample bottle of pills and said, "Dr. Weihen gave me these. He said I need to pay at the desk."

She nodded, took the bottle, and leaned to one side to watch Greenway walk into the office, paper in hand, and shut the door. She billed Turner for the visit and his pills and he signed some papers. She gave him one of the nice pens that she used, not the sad lonely one, because Turner wasn't too bad. He deserved a pen that worked. He mumbled something about sitting down and having another cup of coffee before going out in the cold, but Clara wasn't entirely listening. She was thinking about what Greenway was reading and why he didn't put it away when he walked into Victor's office.

The waiting room soon became crowded. Turner was still sitting there, deep into the black hole that was reality television when the delivery man, Danny, came in to restock the supplies for the month, and for the first time this year. Danny was relatively new, as this was only his second time ever delivering to the office. A few of the items he transported were general office items that the secretary could sign for, but others were private boxes that Victor ordered and requested that only he validate. For some reason, he thought Clara would open them if she signed. As if she cared what he ordered. So she allowed Danny to enter the office to acquire Victor's signature. She didn't mind if he was interrupted.

While Danny was in Victor's office, the front door opened and closed three times. Clara did not have to look up to know it was Mrs. Whittle, an elderly woman with the mind of a thirty year old. She was smart, quick, and very dramatic about everything. She came to the doctor because of her OCD, obsessive compulsive disorder. She nodded to Clara as she gave a little wave, and then sat down precisely two spots away from Turner, as she always needed a chair in between her and others when in the waiting room. Clara didn't want to be rude by staring, so she looked over at Whittle in fragments. The old lady had the eyes of a hawk and would pick up on anything. In the brief seconds that Clara stole a glance, she could see that the woman was uncomfortable. She always sat at the edge of her seat with her hands in her lap, careful not to touch many things. Clearly the doctor wasn't helping her much with her condition.

Danny, after a considerable amount of time for just having Weihen sign a package, left the office and gave a smile as he walked to the door of the waiting room. Clara busied herself with the files as a small anxiety creeped within her. It didn't last long, but the feeling was there.

Greenway opened the door to Victor's office, and the two men exited. Okay. Here came the big deal. He was going to pay his bill. He also had a new bottle of pills, something that would only prolong the process. Victor ushered in Mrs. Whittle as Turner walked out the front door, leaving Clara and Greenway at her desk. Alone.

"Good morning, Clara—"

"Mr. Greenway," she said.

He briefly curled his lip as if he was disgusted before returning to a neutral expression. He handed over the bottle of pills, and Clara entered the information into the computer at a pace equal to that of a superhuman. She watched him carefully as she took his credit card for payment. And then she gave him the papers to sign.

Only the pen that was dried out on the hutch was available for him to use. She made it that way every time *he* signed. As usual, he picked it up, attempted to write and realized it was dry. After a disapproving shake of his head, he dabbed the pen on his tongue and successfully signed the papers. He then left them there and quitted the building. Clara exhaled and slouched her back into the chair. It wasn't comfortable to be around Mitch Greenway, anymore. He was corrupt and foul.

The rest of the work day continued pretty smoothly. Mrs. Whittle talked a lot, but eventually left, and Victor only saw a few patients after that, albeit they were scattered throughout the morning and afternoon. Clara ended up spending several hours at the desk that day.

Memories of the past few months had crept into her mind. She was thinking about her mother, who had made more than a few questionable decisions as of late. She was not entirely sure why the past decided to burrow itself into her brain; she often reminded herself that time only moves forward. It waits for no one. It was a new year, so she shoved history out of her mind. Perhaps it was a year of forgiveness. She was surrounded by people who wronged her, but maybe it was time to move on.

A ring interrupted her thoughts. It was the office phone. The call was unexpected, as there were rarely any calls for Victor. He had a network of patients, and scarcely took new ones on. A patient would have only called to cancel or reschedule, a rare occurrence. The phone rang twice before she answered.

"This is Detective Pearson. May I speak to Dr. Wei-hen?" the voice said.

"I'll put you through."

It was curious that a detective would be calling, but Clara didn't think much of it at the time. She supposed Dr. Weihen should have been the first to know among the two of them, but the news turned out to be infinitely more important to *her*. After a brief few minutes, Victor walked out of his office with a deep furrow on his forehead and teary eyes. She couldn't tell if he was faking or not.

He said, "Mitch Greenway died." He pinched the top of his nose and adjusted the glasses below his monstrous eyebrows. "In fact, he has been murdered."

Chapter Two

*C*lara maintained a slight smile before the meaning behind Victor's words hit her. The doctor even noticed that the grin on her face lingered a bit too long as she struggled to process the new information. After losing balance much too gracefully, she fell into her padded leather office chair, causing it to roll back ever so slightly. She could hardly remember what was going through her mind—an ounce of fright seeped into the emotional part of her brain and a million questions arose. She just couldn't quite understand; death is one thing, but he was *murdered*. It wasn't a question or a suspicion. It rolled off the doctor's tongue as if he was simply requesting her to cancel an appointment. Naturally, she composed herself from the initial state of shock and inquired for more details. Admittedly, she was a bit churlish to Victor, but he would have been the same way.

Clara said, "What could you mean by saying that? You're telling me a man, who I just saw this morning, has died and someone has already come to the conclusion it was murder? Do you think I am a fool?"

"Clara, all I was told is what I have said. The phone call with the detective was very short. I realize death is unusual to hear about. It is almost surreal," he said. "That great man in there was a patient of mine for a long time. Do not get angry with me."

Great man. Clara's muscles tensed. It took a substantial amount of self control to hold back her anger at those words. Mitch Greenway was as sleazy as they came; she would never consider him great. After giving some half-apology to Victor to get him to calm down, she sought the little information he had.

He said, "The detective will be here shortly to take fingerprints and allow us to fill him in on Mitch's actions while he was here. Apparently, it will help with determining 'how' and 'who'." His expression looked helpless. "I cannot believe he was murdered."

The idea that the detective was going to talk to them induced the weird guilt Clara suddenly felt that day. A man she had known all her life, and had come to actually hate, died. They were no longer part of the same world, and something about that did not sit right. His death somehow gave her an advantage over him that left Clara dissatisfied. She was the one who lived—the stronger of the two.

In truth, she worried that because she hated Greenway, she would be a prime suspect in his demise. Clara calmed herself with the idea that absolutely no one knew of her tiny hatred. A mere dislike, really. Victor didn't know, and the detective certainly wouldn't know. She could keep this small detail to herself and bring it with her to the grave. But her heart raced—wouldn't she be withholding information, or worse, *evidence*? No, it wasn't evidence. It was simply a fact. Many people hate people. Not many people murder people.

Besides, the detective couldn't be concerned with the office. Greenway passed away somewhere else, at a later time, or Clara would have seen a body. The inanimate form of Mitch Greenway. She trembled ever so slightly.

The doctor's complexion was graying. Was he upset or nervous? The detective could believe that the victim's psychiatrist poisoned him with pills, or persuaded him to commit the act himself. Anything was possible to the detective. He didn't know Victor or her. He could believe it was a joint operation! She shouldn't have jumped to conclusions. It only made the situation more confusing.

She needed to prepare what she would say. A cold, steady retelling of the events that took place that morning. *Tell the truth, and nothing more*, she said to herself. They didn't need to know she hated him, they just needed to know the facts. She looked around her desk and arranged everything in an orderly fashion. Nothing was out of place or looked bad until she focused her gaze on the pen. It was a good enough day as any for the pen to finally stop wreaking havoc on people with its inability to actually write. Clara almost felt bad for the writing utensil because it was completely useless, and although she tried to keep it functioning, its ugliness eventually caused its own reckoning. She held it in her hands carefully, and was about to throw it in the trash when she realized there was no bag in the bin. Of course, she had forgotten to bring garbage bags. Another item to add to the checklist. She ended up wrapping the tip in a tissue and sticking it in her back pocket. She would throw it out later.

There were no appointments left in the day when the detective arrived. Victor was doing the half of his job that wasn't seeing patients: diagnosing and planning treatments for them. He rose from his work at the first sound of the door. Clara flipped her hair one last time and pretended to act casual. She had never met a detective before.

As the door opened more and more, the image of a man appeared. He was wearing a navy business suit that was just a little too big for him. The pants draped slightly over his shoes. His old tie looked as if it used to be a very pleasant shade of red, but now shared closer resemblance to a brick in the rain. His shoes were too shiny for the rest of his appearance, and he had dark sunglasses over his eyes. As he stepped forward into the room, he went through the motions of holding the door for someone. A second man, much younger, entered.

The blue-suited cop said, "Good afternoon. Is this Dr. Weihen's office?" He wasn't looking at Clara or the doctor, but was generally gazing around the room.

"I am Dr. Weihen. It is nice to meet you, officer," Victor muttered, politely shaking the man's hand.

"Detective Pearson. And this is my partner, Suds." The partner gave a small wave.

After introductions, general conversation about the cold weather, and offerings of coffee and water, the investigation began. They wanted to speak with the doctor and secretary separately, which was already a bad sign. They clearly suspected something and Clara was sure they expected more information from Victor. They spoke to her first.

They were in the therapy room, with Victor outside. Clara sat in his chair and the two policeman sat on the couch. Bracing for a long interview, she found herself relaxed and even slightly annoyed. Part of her day was going to be wasted; she could have left because there were no more patients. One should never have to be interrogated about a murder that just happened, anyway. Irrational thoughts pervade a person's mind and blind the detectives from the truth. But she used her time efficiently to learn more about the murder.

Pearson broke the initial silence. "This must be strange news for you, uh, Miss—"

"Tulit. Clara Tulit."

"Okay Ms. Tulit. How are you holding up?"

"Well, as a matter of fact, I find it extremely odd that a man died only a few hours ago and you have already come to the conclusion that he was murdered."

"Yes, well, Ms. Tulit, we take our jobs very seriously. We're very good at what we do. Now we don't know if it was murder… ehrm, or suicide… but we certainly know that he did not die naturally, as they say."

"And how did he die exactly?"

The two detectives looked at each other hesitantly. Pearson said, "We believe it was from poison. A very lethal type of poison—it only takes a drop until…But of course, we're awaiting the coroner's confirmation."

They already knew the weapon. Poison. The events of the morning flashed through Clara's head to detect any moments where Mitch Greenway could have been poisoned. She couldn't think of anything. He walked in, ignored her, and went in with Victor. He never even had any coffee! The only way he was poisoned here was if Victor did it when they were alone. But that was impossible. Mitch Greenway would have died in this very office if that were the case. Or so she believed.

She needed more answers. "How did you know it was poison?"

Pearson gave a proud pat on his partner's shoulder. Clara had forgotten about the partner until then. He was quiet and faded into the background. Pearson said, "Little Suds here knows all. One of the smartest on our team. We agreed the man looked too healthy to die and well, there weren't any other signs for causes of death. Suds came to some smart conclusions."

Suds chimed, "But you see, it wasn't his health that guided me to poison. He could have had a minor stroke or heart attack, and still *look* normal. Nothing is certain until the coroner does an examination." He paused. "I had the faintest feeling it was poison from the victim's face. One would think that he would look shocked or frightened. But he wasn't. No, in the extremely brief moments between pain and death, there is a look of realization. Greenway had that expression. Whether he was murdered or not, he quickly understood he was going to die."

His argument for poison was flimsy at best, and so Clara subconsciously labeled Suds as "foolish" in her mind. It might have been a mistake. He certainly sounded like he had no idea what he was doing, but she had no idea if he was really intelligent or not. And after all, he would later be correct about the poison. His reasoning seemed awfully flawed, though.

Pearson said, "You see? The kid is pretty smart. You know how he got the name Suds?"

She really did not want to know, but indulged him. "How?"

He said, "It was his first case, our first job together. It was only a year ago, I suppose. We arrived on the scene and it was a bloody mess. The guy was nailed a few times in the back with a meat slicing knife." Clara vomited in her mouth a little bit. "Anyway, after looking over the scene, we found a startlingly little amount of evidence. No fingerprints, no hairs, nothing. We couldn't even tell if he was right-handed or left-handed because the wounds told us he was both! Everything was clean. The murder weapon was still there, but the only fingerprints on it were from the victim himself. I looked over at Suds, and I told him that this case wasn't going to last very long. There just wasn't enough to go on. He looked around and then asked me, 'But where's the soap?' Now, I didn't know what he was talking about then, but he made the case that if the killer was so clean, he probably would have washed his hands. And well, there was no soap at the only sink at the scene of the crime. There weren't any cleaning materials at all. No sponges. Nothing. All gone. It's pretty hard to wash off blood with no soap! And as it turns out, after doing a search, we found a bottle of antibacterial soap and a whole mess of towels in the trash can of a gas station two miles out. No fingerprints, but the gas station had cameras! That was Suds' first case. I was pretty impressed. Now I trust him and his little ideas."

He was laughing and looking at Suds, who was looking at Clara. She didn't quite know how to respond. Was he really that brilliant? Wouldn't anyone think the first thing to do is see how the killer cleaned up? It seemed like Suds had nothing more than a lucky hunch.

When they finally got around to actually interviewing her, they asked the big question. *Describe the events of the day.* Clara gave a pretty short response for something that was probably important.

"Well, I came to work early because it was the first day back from the holidays. When I got there, Dr. Weihen was sleeping on the couch of his office. After I woke him up and prepared the office, the patients soon came. First, Leiman Turner. Then," she gulped, "Mitch Greenway. Then Mrs. Whittle, of course. I supposed you'd like me to focus on Mr. Greenway. He walked in, stayed just a few minutes in the waiting room, and then went into see Dr. Weihen. After, he came out, quickly signed his forms, and left. That was all I saw of him."

Pearson tapped his pen, refraining from writing anything. He asked, "Was there anything unusual about him? Did he look sad or angry? Was he wearing or holding anything unordinary?"

Clara thought briefly. He didn't acknowledge her, but he never did. He was covered from top to bottom in dark clothing, but he always did that to disguise himself. Eventually, something peculiar came to mind. She said, "You know, he had some papers in his hands. He took them out of his briefcase and was reading them in the waiting room. He usually reads a magazine, but that's not what caused my suspicion. I remember thinking it strange that he never put the papers back in his briefcase. He took them into the office with him. Maybe it's nothing, I really don't know."

Suds asked, "You didn't see what was on these papers?"

"No, sir, if there is one thing you should know about me—I am not a *snooper*. I don't eavesdrop, and I certainly don't try to read papers that aren't mine!"

Pearson said, "We didn't think you would. It was merely a question, ma'am. I think you've answered just about everything we need to know from you."

He got up, opened the door, and ushered her out. Clara left the room. What a disappointment. She didn't really give that much information, so she wasn't a valuable contribution to the investigation. And she wanted more answers. It was too late, because she was already at her desk when the door closed to Victor's office. It was his turn to comply.

Clara didn't know what to do while they were in the office. She wanted to know what Victor was saying and if they were giving him any more information. No one wants to give the secretary any information, but the esteemed doctor who has been caring for the deceased for years? He must know something.

She was already standing next to the door. Carefully, without a sound, she moved to be directly in front of it. She pressed her left ear to the wood and focused hard. The effort was entirely unnecessary, however, because she found that their loud voices could be heard quite clearly. Nevertheless, she gently kept her ear there. Victor was talking.

"He was out of his normal prescription of antidepressant, so I gave him a sample I had in the office. He was supposed to take it this morning, but he wanted to wait until he got home. He says it makes him tired, so he wanted to be at a place where he could sleep." Clara didn't know if that was true or not.

"I see," Pearson said. "Dr. Weihen, let me provide you with some of the details here that Suds and I are worried about. Greenway left your office at around eleven in the morning. Only a half-hour later, at eleven thirty, he is found lifeless in the entryway of his mansion. Now, there is no evidence that he made any stops between your office and home. I do not believe that a moral man like you committed this act of horror, but the facts don't look very good for you."

Clara swallowed the lump in her throat. His last remark was both comforting and damning. The detectives didn't believe he did it, but the evidence was unmatched. She felt uneasy that the future of this case and Victor's innocence lay entirely in the hands of these two detectives. One that sometimes had a good hunch, and the other that praised his partner for every easy thing he does.

The idea had come. Perhaps she could lead an investigation herself. It would be no easy feat, but she could bring the person who was guilty to justice. The person who would answer and be punished for the crime. Not to save Victor—she couldn't care less about him—but to remove a real criminal from society. And she desperately wanted to know who killed Mitch Greenway.

Clara stopped listening but was still standing at the door when it opened. She was as surprised to be hit by the door as Pearson was to see her behind it.

She hesitated, but quickly said, "Sorry, I was going to knock. Did you want any more water?"

"No," he said. "Thank you."

He believed her. A relief. But then Suds walked out and whispered, "You don't eavesdrop, huh?"

Clara's face flushed as he followed his partner out the door of the waiting room. Just as he walked out, he turned around and gave a playful smile at her. She waved goodbye, and he left. Suds was very strange and his attitude was a cause for concern.

At the sound of the door closing, she walked into Victor's office to find him sitting at his desk and looking as if he was turned to stone. His face was pale and he was breathing fast. He must have been thinking about what the detectives said.

Clara said, "I'm going home. There's no more patients today."

For the first time in the eight months that she worked for him, he gave her a compliment. "Good work, Clara. I'm afraid this office won't be open much longer, however."

She rolled her eyes. She just wanted to go home after this awful day, and now she had to console Victor Weihen, a person unworthy of her sympathy. Yet in the realization that she might go home quicker if she complied, she said, "Don't worry, Victor. You didn't do anything to Mitch Greenway. Pearson and Suds know that."

"Yes, yes. I'm afraid that I am guilty, however, in a way. I gave him those pills, and anyone could have dipped them in poison. If I didn't give them to him, he probably wouldn't have died."

Clara said, "Don't say that. Who knows if the poison was on the pills, anyway? He could have sipped or eaten anything in a half hour's worth of time. Don't worry, I'll find out who really deserves to answer for this crime."

And so she made a promise. An unrealistic promise. It may have been to Victor, but it was out there. She would begin her personal investigation as soon as the next day. She left Victor in his state of guilt, and didn't feel bad for it for one second. She was excited to take on the role of a detective. Like a heroine in a thriller novel, except she was selfish. Pure curiosity drove her, not entirely justice. She did not have the sense of "moral compass" that sleuths so often possessed. And if she ended up saving Victor, perhaps it was because she just wanted to keep her job. She left the office into the unusual cold. The car ride home was only five minutes, but that day, it felt like hours.

Chapter Three

As Clara was driving home, she reflected on the events of the day. A normal day at the office... until a patient that seemed completely fine died. This was also no ordinary patient. This was Mitch Greenway. The thought hadn't occurred to her yet—*Mitch Greenway* was murdered! He was a billionaire; he was famous. It was going to be all over the news. Victor Weihen's name would surely be mentioned. Her name might be mentioned! After all, she did speak to the detectives. She was a witness to Greenway's whereabouts prior to his demise.

A new idea entered her mind. It was a revelation of sorts. Greenway *was* a billionaire, so the murderer might have been after his money. Could it have been in the family? An internal affair? He had a wife, Linda, and a son, Miles, both of whom would have received inheritance. Though, neither of them would make very good suspects (unless, of course, the motive wasn't financial). Clara knew them all, and they were certainly not being excluded from the money. Miles wore expensive, tailored clothing every time she saw him and Linda, well, she often toted her multiple pearl necklaces and gold earrings. Not to mention she was presumably never without her diamond wedding ring—estimated to be worth millions, though Clara never asked her the real cost. Certainly, Victor couldn't be that convincing of a suspect when he had no monetary gains. Actually, Victor didn't really have anything to gain at all.

Clara temporarily forgot the issues of the day as she rounded her street corner. She lived with her mom and sister in a small house in the museum district of Houston. She used to have so many things going for her— straight A's in high school, the best violinist in the orchestra— but she eventually could not take the pressure anymore. She was at a big, fancy university when her attention started to decline. The intelligence was still there, but passion was lost... or forgotten. She moved back home and attended a community college for a while. Then, she gave it up altogether and did nothing but live in her mother's house for the next year. After a long job search, she became a secretary to the doctor. Clara couldn't help but think her sister followed in her footsteps. She, too, was a dropout and did nothing with her privileges.

As the car rolled down the street, the trees that Clara loved so much were in full view. They were beautiful to look at, with huge branches resembling spiderwebs. They were as if an artist crafted their design, the branches all intricately woven together, with sharp angles that one wouldn't normally see on a tree. The large plants lined the street and she remembered when she was little, all of the kids on the block would think it was a competition for who had the best tree on their property. It wasn't hers.

She pulled into the driveway and got out of the small Subaru. It was still light outside, but the lights in the house were on. That meant Clara's sister was home. She would turn them on, regardless, and it would drive their mom crazy because it wasted energy and was bad for the environment. Clara walked in, only to hear the television blasting.

"Hey," she said.

Her sister—Tracy—was on the couch, eyes glued to the damn thing. She always had a small frame, so she took up almost no space curled up amongst the pillows. She was just two years younger than Clara, and looked much different. She had blond hair; Clara had brown. She had small, beady eyes; Clara's were large, but hid behind her glasses. She wore loose comfortable clothing and Clara often wore business attire. A news channel screamed out of the flatscreen. Clara could hear the awful jumble of noise that one hears when a newscaster is speaking, but she wasn't listening. Every male newscaster sounded exactly the same.

She put her keys in the tray and hung up her coat.

"Where's mom?"

Again, no answer. To be fair, it wasn't a great question, though. Mom would be in the kitchen or in her bedroom. So Clara tried the kitchen.

"Clara, good that you're here. Have you seen the new red lipstick I bought the other day?"

Her mom was searching through drawers. Clara was rather unconcerned where she had misplaced her lipstick. Her purse was open on the counter.

"I don't know, mom. Have you checked your purse?"

26

The frantic woman closed a drawer and looked up at Clara. "Yes, that was the first place I checked! Oh, I really liked that lipstick. It made me look, I don't know, power-ful." She was touching her lips with her fingers. Her eyes were on something else, not Clara.

Her dress was short and black. She had a few gold bangles on her wrist and her hair looked like it was nicely washed and blown dry. She was wearing four-inch heals to compensate for her height. Clara knew what her mom was doing, but wasn't going to say anything. She wanted her to open up about it first. Her mom had been dressing up and going out a few times a week for the past few months. It was obvious she was seeing someone. Clara didn't know what she was going to do tonight, however. How would she take the news? She had been friends with Greenway for a long time. She wouldn't hear about a friend's death and then go out on a date.

"You're dressed up, mom. Are you going some-where?"

"Oh, just the book club, sweetie. I just really wanted that lipstick."

The book club was her usual excuse. Often it was just a night out with "friends," or sometimes she even lied about it being a blind date. Funny how she never sees those blind dates again.

"Why don't you go out to dinner with your sister?" she offered.

Clara said, "I think we'll order in or something. I'm too tired. A long day." She was itching to reveal the news, but her mom was in a self-obsessed state, not having the courtesy to ask about her own daughter's day. Clara had to say it eventually. It would just come out. But she would wait until they were all in the same room, so Tracy can hear too. She's be interested. Mitch was just an acquaintance to Tracy and Clara, but they *knew* him. He was one of those family friends you just don't care enough for.

Clara left her mom in the kitchen and went upstairs. She knew her mother wouldn't be leaving for another hour or so. She went into her room and started to undress. She felt sore and sick. The quintessential feelings when death invades a person's life.

When she was taking off her pants, she noticed something inside them. she felt around and found the pen from the office in the pocket. It was wrapped in a tissue. She must have forgotten about it. She was going to throw it out, but figuring it should continue its existence as a pen, she threw out the tissue and placed the utensil in the black cupholder on her childhood desk. She then proceeded into the bathroom and started a hot shower. It was necessary to decompress from the events of the day. How could so much happen in roughly seven hours? A man dies, and detectives are already going around asking people questions. Clara didn't know much about forensics, but wouldn't it be a bit longer for them to find out he was murdered? Oh wait, they had Suds. He apparently knew everything. Clara laughed as she stepped over the side of the tub, drew back the curtain, and felt the heat rush over her skin.

Her best thinking happened in the shower, but it was wasted as she grappled with the idea of death. Would it mean anything to anyone outside her immediate family if she died? She read somewhere that a person experiences two deaths. The first is when that person physically dies—heart stops, blood loses oxygen, brain stops working, and so on. The second is the last time that person is ever mentioned or thought of by another. It is when one's existence is never further acknowledged by humanity. Plenty of people have died and sadly, plenty of people have had their second deaths. But many people haven't. Everyone still knows Caesar, Shakespeare, various Egyptian pharaohs and others. It will take a long time for these names to be forgotten. Mitch Greenway would not be lost, either. His family would think about him for generations, and his name would surface when discussing the ruthlessness of oil companies. Clara? Well, her family would think of her and maybe a few friends. She had no lovers or kids and probably wouldn't ever have any, so it seems her second death will be when her mother, sister, and few friends die. Clara pushed death out of her mind. It was no use to think about it.

Instead, she created a list of suspects. Who did she know who was near Greenway and could have had the opportunity to slip poison into him or his pills? Well, there was Victor of course. But there were also several patients. Leiman Turner, who possibly had depression? She wasn't sure. Mrs. Whittle, the obsessive compulsive woman. Clara herself, who she doubted would be suspicious to the police, but it was important to keep in mind. And that delivery man, Danny. Those were the people in the office. Other possible suspects could be Miles and Linda. Were either of them at the house when he returned home? *Did* he return home? Yes, he was found in the entryway. By who? Further investigation was needed.

Clara turned off the faucet and grabbed a towel. After drying off, she slipped into a pair of comfortable sweatpants and a loose shirt. She threw on her glasses and noticing the time, went downstairs. The shower lasted longer than expected. Mom would be leaving in about ten minutes. She heard some loud exclamation as she got to the bottom of the staircase and saw her mother rushing through the hallway holding a small cosmetic.

"I found it, Clara! The lipstick!" She waltzed by her daughter and into the bathroom. Clara didn't respond and continued through the hallway into the living room, where Tracy was still watching the television.

She half noticed that Clara entered the room and flatly said, "Oh such sad news. Very sad. I can't stand when things like this happen."

For a moment, Clara thought that Greenway's murder might have already been on the news. She walked in and looked at the TV. She wanted to be the one to reveal the news to her, especially since she was involved. She liked to be dramatic that way. Besides, she didn't want Tracy to feel like she lied to her by not saying anything. A wave of relief hit her when she saw some news story about a bus crashing. Four fatalities. Awful, but not as awful as *murder*.

Mom walked in just then and her lips looked like a vampire's after dinner. She sat down, putting the lipstick back in her purse, and glanced carelessly at the television.

She said, "Tracy, don't watch these things. They are much too depressing."

Tracy turned the volume low, and then switched the channel. She was ready to converse with the family. It was time.

"So I had a very unfortunate day at work." Tracy looked over, her eyes gesturing to go on. Her mother was still shifting around in her purse, but she was listening. Clara continued, "One of the doctor's patients was murdered." She said it casually, but began the waterworks soon after. She swallowed a big gulp of air and started to fake a small cry. It would have been odd if she hadn't. "And you'll never guess who."

Tracy sat up, and mom closed her purse. They were both very intrigued.

Tracy finally said, "How terrible! Who?"

Clara positioned herself for the big reveal. This was going to be all the news in Houston for the next few weeks, and she was going to tell them firsthand. Tracy was a trained gossip, loving anything and everything about scandal and murder. Mom, well, she was undoubtedly going to respond quite appropriately. Clara took a deep breath and said, "Mitch Greenway!"

Clara watched her mom. The purse slipped off the woman's lap in a momentary burst of emotion. She composed herself just quick enough for Tracy not to notice. She saw that Clara noticed.

Blushing, her mom said, "Oh, my goodness. That's… that's… no good. He was such a good friend of mine." Her voiced was wavering and sadness filled her eyes. "You girls grew up with Miles. I can't believe it. Oh dear." She picked up her handbag, shaking her head.

Tracy didn't show her normal form of excitement to news like this. Instead, a faint tear developed in her eye. It wasn't the expected reaction, but at least she was showing some empathy. She would normally be interested.

Maybe it was a bit too personal this time. Tracy read all those detective novels. Clara was even thinking about asking her to join in the secret investigation. But her sister looked confused, upset.

She asked, "How do you know he was murdered?"

Clara explained the story. The early day at the office, the call from the police, and the detectives. She even went into the backstory of the detectives, about Suds and his skills for a rookie. She got no reaction from Tracy, though. Mom looked uncomfortable, maybe even disappointed. Naturally, she didn't say anything.

"Do the police know who did it?" Tracy asked. She was getting her inquisitiveness back.

"No, but there are several suspects," Clara tried to entice her. "Several people were in the office this morning, and then of course there is familial motive."

"Yes, there's that," she said, eyes wide.

Tracy was beginning to be curious about the case. Maybe she would help after all. But now was not the time to ask. Clara diverted her attention to their mom. She was fidgeting and acting very strangely.

Clara said, "Mom, are you okay?"

She looked up and said, "Oh yes, everything is fine." Her fingers were tapping to an unheard rhythm. She looked at her watch and got up from her seat. "I really have to be getting to book club."

It was a lie. Yet she walked out the door and drove away. *How could she leave?* Clara didn't know when she would be back but for some reason, she knew it would be soon. She was left with her sister in the living room. Tracy had recovered from her initial state of shock, and began asking questions.

"Was Greenway acting strangely? Did the police say anything about his family? I wonder what Linda and Miles think. Who does the money go to?" She continued on and on.

Clara rested her head on the cushion. "I don't know, Tracy. All I know is that he died. He was murdered. Poison, apparently."

"Poison?" She jumped up. Her nervous face returned for just a moment, but vanished quickly. She said, "How fascinating!" Though her eyes told a different story. She was clearly preoccupied with something else.

"You know, I was thinking about conducting my own little investigation. I think the police suspect Victor, but I don't believe he did it for a second. Still, I need to make sure that justice is served to the correct person."

She was excited for the inquiry and wanted to help. Clara thought she might, so she told her she would let her know all the facts that accumulate, and they could figure it out together. Clara often tried to involve her sister in things because not much goes on in Tracy's life. She dropped out of college and was unemployed. She mainly just sat in the house, reading or watching television. Clara felt bad that she had nothing going on.

After it was decided she would be a consulting detective of sorts, Clara said, "Now, what do you want to eat?"

The next hour or so consisted of them watching television, waiting for their food to arrive, and eating. They decided on Mexican food. Tex-Mex. It was truly the best. Clara always got fish tacos, and Tracy always got beef enchiladas. Guacamole and chips, of course, were always a necessity.

Tracy said, "Hey, so I was thinking about maybe getting a job." *Here we go again.* She made this statement every other week and it never came to fruition.

Clara rolled her eyes, half-laughing, knowing even Tracy thought it was a joke at this point. "Yes, and where will that job be?"

Tracy ignored her playful, mocking attitude and said, "I was thinking I could do something at the zoo. You know, take care of animals and all that."

Clara took a bite of my fish taco and stared at her sister. There was a perfectly timed pause, then they both broke out laughing. Bits of fish and beef went over their plates and they put their hands to their mouths.

"The zoo? You're crazy. You're allergic to about every animal that has hair."

She was still catching her breath. "Well, they might have hypoallergenic animals these days. It's common."

"What are you talking about? I've heard of a hypoallergenic dog, not a hypoallergenic lion."

They both continued to laugh, and then turned the television volume back up. Some police detective drama bullshit show was on when they saw the headlights outside the window. Mom was back. Tracy didn't really think anything of it, but Clara knew it was a little too early for book club to have ended. She rested her taco.

The girls' mom walked in and was bawling. Makeup was all over her face and she dropped her purse onto the floor. She rushed into the living room, where Tracy and Clara were. Tracy immediately got up and hugged her, asking her what was wrong, and Clara tried to look concerned. They both sat down on the couch.

Her mother said, "Clara, could I have some water?"

Clara heard more crying as she went to the kitchen, quickly grabbing a foggy glass out of the cabinet, and putting it under the faucet. It was warm water, so she dumped it into the sink and refilled it with cold. She was anxious to get back into the room and hear what her mother had to say.

Clara reentered and handed her mom the glass. She took a big sip and placed it onto the wooden coffee table. There were bright red lipstick marks where she had put her mouth.

She took in a breath and said, "Girls, I have something to admit to you. Something very important. Please, I beg of you, do not judge me." Her eyes were wide and filled with tears. Clara was thinking about how Tracy would respond.

"What is it, mom?" her sister asked.

"Well, you see, I have been *seeing* Mitch Greenway for some time now." She paused. "That is, we had been having an affair. I was his mistress." Her crying had relapsed.

Tracy's jaw dropped. Clara tried to give a convincing look of shock, but it was certainly no surprise to her.

Chapter Four

*I*t was the beginning of November when Clara had first learned of the rather odd relationship between her mother and Greenway. She knew something was going on before that, but didn't know *what* or *who*. It was the birth of a new era for her mom: she would be going out at strange times during the night, wearing disturbingly tight clothing and lipsticks with exotic colors meant for middle school girls. Usually a "girls' night out" with the occasional "book club." Clara paid no attention to it, figuring it was one of those crises that are so often talked about. She was past her midlife, but is there really only one crisis to look forward to?

The Greenways were family friends. Unbelievably, a billionaire family was actually associated with Clara's mediocre family. They weren't poor—her father made an honest living as a banker—but they lived modestly, despite their reasonable wealth. A small house near the museums was more manageable for her mom and dad. As children, Tracy and Clara were never given many toys or clothes. Yet, they both went to a rich prep school filled with pretentious heirs. One of them was Miles Greenway.

Miles was different from the rest of the snobs. He was funny, down-to-earth, and seemed genuine—like a real person. He was in the year below Clara, the one above her sister. Clara's mom had also gone to the same college as Mitch, and after learning they grew up and lived in the same town as each other, they became pretty good friends. Family dinners, celebrations, holidays were all spent with the Greenways. Sometimes at the Tulit house, sometimes at the Greenways' enormous estate.

It was no surprise on that early November day that her mom had said, "The Greenways are coming over for dinner, isn't that fun? They haven't been in ages."

Clara said, "Mitch and Linda?"

"Miles too."

To be honest, Clara couldn't have been more neutral about the Greenways coming over. They were just awkward family friends. Not too exciting. It was different for the "kids," she supposed. She didn't know Miles too well; her sister knew him better. Usually, during these dinners, the parents would mingle, Tracy would be conversing with Miles, and Clara would just be alone. And it continued as they all grew older. It should have been different, but it wasn't.

It's almost impossible to overlook the luxury of the Greenways' lives. They arrived at the house in a black Mercedes. It was glossy and the lights had a controlled brightness that cut through the semidarkness of twilight like an expensive blade.

Mitch got out first, but didn't go around to the other side of the car to help his wife out like he normally did. Instead, Miles emerged from the passenger seat, carrying some sort of food, most likely a dessert (they always brought dessert). They both started toward the front door. Linda wasn't with them.

Clara opened the door before they could ring the bell. Should she give a hug or a formal greeting or what? It had been a long time. So she swooped in to take the tray of cookies from Miles. It backfired, though, because as she grabbed them, he leaned in and gave her a kiss on the cheek. So then, whilst holding the cookies, she had to give Mitch a kiss on his face as well.

"Nice to see you," Clara said.

"All is well, Clara?" Mitch asked. The normal interchanges of friends coming over for dinner. He didn't actually care, but it was something to say. He was looking over Clara's shoulder into the house, as if he was expecting someone else to come. No one did.

"Come in," Clara said. She didn't bother answering his question. She laid the tray of cookies down, and proceeded to take the black camelhair peacoat from Mitch. Miles didn't wear a jacket, not that he had to. It was beautiful November weather. She assumed Mitch just always wore his coat, no matter the weather. She never saw him without it.

Mitch was just saying that he could hang the coat himself when Clara's mother came down the stairs. Clara's eyes widened a bit when she saw her mom's outfit. The dress was dark red, low cut, and wouldn't come close to covering the knees. It was one of those dresses that you pay a ridiculous sum for very little fabric. The lipstick matched the color of the dress, but the rest of her makeup looked overdone (a *lot* of mascara). Perhaps the most shocking part of her outfit was the jewelry. Diamonds on her neck and ears. Clara had never seen them before.

"Mitch, darling. It's been so long." Her voice faltered. It didn't mean anything at the time. She hugged him, and then shook Miles' hand.

Mitch said, "Carin, how are you?"

"Oh, just perfect. So glad you came." She looked around with her eyes, puzzled, but a little too dramatic. She said, "Where's Linda?"

Mitch took the cue. "Oh yes, she had a charity meeting tonight. She's the president of a small charity, you know, called, 'Cooking for a Cause.'"

"So sorry she couldn't make it." She gave the faintest hint of a smile. "Miles, you look so old. I remember when you were just in elementary school with Clara and Tracy. What are you doing these days?"

He recited his usual, polite, charming response. "Not much, just preparing for life." He laughed a little. It was a perfect response for a lazy individual like himself. He didn't do much, like Tracy and Clara. He was more or less just sitting and waiting to inherit the company.

"Sit down, please." Clara's mom motioned towards the living room and everyone walked over in a painfully slow manner. Mitch was the first to reach the couch. Miles cautiously stepped in, acting as if he didn't want to intrude. For some reason, the Greenways looked too big in the Tulit's moderately sized living room. They were used to their own, which was probably the size of two olympic swimming pools. Miles sat next to his father, which brought a sour expression upon her mom's face. Clara had thought she was just being rude.

The following hour was filled with uninteresting, fluffy, mannerly discussion. It was a waste of brain power for Clara, and most likely a loss of it, too. At some point, early on in the awful discussion, Tracy had come down the stairs. She was also in a dress and makeup, but not nearly as bad as her mom. Clara realized that she was the one underdressed in pants and a sweater. Her hair was in a ponytail. She had applied no makeup. It only made it that much more awkward.

Clara was a mere acquaintance with these people. Tracy was more agreeable to Miles. Mom was clearly friends with Mitch. *More* than friends, as Clara would soon find out. Clara just didn't fit in. Her instinct of being left out was right; she was essentially a third wheel in the whole situation.

Dinner was finally ready, but much too late. Clara's mom did this terrible thing of purposely starting the food when the guests arrived, so that it would take forever to eat. That way, the guests would stay longer. She really was desperate for company, especially after the girls' dad died.

Despite a fairly large dining room, the table was quite small. It often only had four chairs surrounding it—perfect for the family. They had to add another makeshift chair, making the whole thing look sloppy. Of course, Clara sat in the makeshift chair, so people naturally believed it was her fault. The food was appetizing, of course. Mom was always a good cook. Mitch was hamming up the dish.

He said, "Carin, I don't know how you do it. My grandmother always made a roast, and I thought it was the best in the world at the time. But it doesn't even compare to yours." He winked at her. She blushed. How could Clara not realize what was going on just then? Miles, too, gave a strange look. He wasn't thinking anything of it, though. Or was he? Did *he* know?

The meal went as usual: mom got a little tipsy, Mitch kept pouring her more wine, and Miles eventually gave Tracy that "Wanna get outta here?" look. It was just like when they were kids, minus Linda. Tracy and Miles left, and after about twenty minutes, Clara followed them into the living room. She just couldn't listen to Mitch and her mother anymore. They were probably relieved when she left, anyway.

The "kids" each had a glass of wine in hand and mutually decided to turn on the television. They settled on some show about a police officer. Shockingly, the cop didn't play by the rules. Tracy was into it, Miles seemed quite disinterested. Clara found the whole plot of it ridiculous. Officer Dickson sets up elaborate, vulnerable traps in order to catch the criminals he's after. In this episode, he was forcing a woman to isolate herself on an empty sidewalk (and eventually walk into a dark alley) in order to draw in her rapist. The particular perpetrator had a habit of stalking his prey, and striking his object more than once.

Miles commented, "The trap is too cliché. No psychopath would fall for it, they're too smart."

Tracy, without diverting her gaze from the screen, said, "Not all psychopaths are smart. And not all rapists are psychopaths."

"Of course they are!"

"No, I read it in a book."

41

It was true. Victor was fascinated in psychopathy. He never had a patient that exhibited symptoms, though, or at least he never told Clara about any. He said only a handful of criminals are psychopaths, most of them are normal. Most of them feel bad for what they have done, and therefore, show empathy. Psychopaths show no empathy. Clara wondered if Victor had lied to her. It always seemed his office might have had a few crazies.

The episode was just coming to an end. Dickson's scheme didn't go according to plan. The rapist apparently wasn't there to abuse the girl, he was there to kill her. Before Dickson could pop out and arrest him, the guy shot the woman dead. It ended with Dickson questioning his skills, blah blah blah. All of these shows were the same. They used the power of shock and nothing else to entice audiences. Clara drank her last sip of wine and left the living room to grab a refill.

She went straight to the kitchen and searched for the bottle. It was on the counter in the middle of a cluster of dirty dishes. She started to pour when she heard a noise upstairs. Curious, she checked the living room and no one was there. It was strange that mom *and* Mr. Greenway would have gone upstairs, she thought, so she decided to check it out, bringing the glass of wine with her.

Clara ascended the stairs slowly—the house creaked much too often, something that had always bothered her. The stairs were especially loud, so she kept to the side of them, thinking the squeaks were more toward the middle of the steps. She made it up with no noises, and went over to the door of her mom's bedroom. It was opened just slightly. Clara couldn't see anything, but she could certainly hear. Giggles and sucking.

"Oh, Mitch, darling. It's been too long."

"Only a week, my dear." A kiss. A deep, awful laugh.

"When will it be time to run away, Mitch? To leave Houston and family pressures and Linda? When will we just pack up and leave?"

"It's complicated, Carin." A kiss. "Where shall we go?"

"An island… in South America! No, too close. France. Marseilles, oh Mitch! Let's go to Marseilles."

"Oui, oui." Then he gave some interpretation of a French laugh. "*Hon hon hon..*"

Clara couldn't listen to it anymore. It was horrifying. The wine dropped from her hand. She couldn't tell if she did it on purpose, subconsciously, or she was really too shocked to grip anything. Either way, it fell on the thin carpet and made a thud. There was a puddle of red beneath her feet. She heard them jump from the sound. Shit, she thought.

The door opened a few moments later. Mom's lipstick was slightly smudged, but faded. She must have tried to wipe it away. She looked at the stain, and then at Clara. Her eyebrows raised in confusion, and her lips were moving. She was surely conjuring up her excuse. Quite a lot of brain activity for her.

She said, "Oh, Clara. What did you do?" She kneeled and picked the glass off the floor.

Clara said, "I—I was just going to my room. I needed to plug my phone into the charger."

"Your room is down the hall, honey," she said, concerned.

"I'm a bit disoriented." She gave a little motion as if she were chugging something, implying she was drinking a bit too much. "What are you doing up here?" She slurred her speech to be more accurate.

"Oh, well—Um. I was just showing Mitch my collection of Japanese folding fans. He seemed very interested."

"Where is Mitch?" Clara's voice faltered a bit.

"In the bathroom… he's um, in the bathroom. He's feeling a little ill, sweetie. Why don't we go downstairs and leave him alone?" She said it loud, so he could hear through the door.

The rest of the night consisted of Clara thinking while everyone else acted normal. She couldn't say anything. Her mom stared at her from time to time, but eventually stopped and forgot about the whole thing. Clara decided she would have to keep a watch on her mom and Mitch. She wouldn't ruin anything, but make sure they were secretive enough. If this got into the news, the papers, Mitch would lose, but not nearly as much as the Tulits. They would be rejected by society. They weren't powerful enough.

Yes, Clara was going to track the whole relationship. It was the beginning of an awful series of discoveries. Affairs were wicked things. Full of betrayal. And this one would lead straight to Mitch Greenway's death. She was quite sure. One way or another, the murder had to be connected to the affair, right? His lies were what killed him.

For the entire night, there was a little voice inside her head that wouldn't go away. It was saying, *"Hon hon hon…"*

* * *

Clara's mom was crying as she found her way to the couch. She threw her purse on the pillow, and papers flew out, but she or Tracy didn't acknowledge them. She slumped over and began sobbing. She was desperately trying to save face with her daughters.

Tracy said, "Mom, what are you talking about? You had an affair with Mitch Greenway? You didn't tell us?"

Their mother didn't look up. She let out an atrocious sound that resembled pain. "I'm sorry, girls. It has... you know, it's been so hard since your father passed. Women have needs, you see, you know that. I didn't think anyone would want me anymore. I'm fifty five, for God's sake! Life was going too fast. He always loved me. I didn't always love him. But we just... we just reconnected lately. He listened to me, I saw passion in his eyes. Please, please... forgive me." She looked up and met Clara's eyes. Clara nodded her head, as if it was obligatory. She had to forgive her. There was too much at stake—she needed to make sure she wasn't a suspect for the recent crime. Obviously, it wasn't her. But she was a mistress! Guilty in the eyes of detectives. Pearson would fish her out. But how could he? She made sure no one knew about the affair. She made sure.

Tracy went over to her mom and held her hand. "Of course we can forgive you. It's not like you cheated on anyone. Dad's dead, you could do anything you want." Odd choice of words. Rather heartless. She continued, "Tell us the story. From the beginning. We will help you."

The crying lady looked up, scared. "No, honey, it's between Mitch and me. Leave it at that. Not another soul needs to know." She wasn't going to say anything more. So far, no one knew the *rest* of the story. Besides Clara. But that would be best left a secret. She just needed to make sure Pearson or Suds didn't get a hold of it.

Tracy let out a few tears. She was too emotional. It was really hard listen to it, but Clara sat down anyway. She wanted to see what those papers were in her mom's purse. When she picked them up, her eyes widened. She had forgotten about this. So stupid. It was obvious it would come out.

"Mom, what the hell are these?"

She stuttered but managed to say, "Oh, Clara, you don't understand..."

Outraged, Clara said, "I'll tell you what they are. Plane tickets. To Marseilles! Is this a joke? When were you going to tell us you were vacationing to France?"

"It was just a quick trip. We wanted to leave..."

"*We*? Who else were you going with, exactly?" She knew exactly who, but wanted to hear her mother say it out loud.

She gulped. "Mitch. We were going to go to Marseilles."

The senselessness! The selfishness! "I can't believe it, mom. Do you know how bad this looks? They need to be gone! Mitch is dead! Did *you* kill him?"

She stood up, angry. "Clara, you know I didn't! We were going to leave this place for a little while. Just for two weeks. We would be back before anyone started questioning. We both wanted to do this." It wasn't a

46

mutual decision. It was a wild dream of her mother's. Mitch was never actually going to go.

Clara said, "We need to get rid of them."

She said, "I was thinking about it. There was no book club tonight. I was driving around aimlessly to find a good place to throw them away. I couldn't think of one."

"Thank God you didn't. They need to be burned, you see. Oh, what's the use? The airline has records of them! The detectives will find these immediately."

She put her hands on Clara. "Clara, listen to me. No one knows anything about this affair. They won't be looking for airline tickets made out to me. Besides, check the name."

Clara looked. The tickets were under a pseudonym. Abigail Richmond. For once, the cleverness of her mother shined through.

Chapter Five

"GREENWAY DEAD, INVESTIGATION ENSUES," read the front page of the newspaper. It was the morning after the day he died. Clara still had work—Victor wasn't going to close shop just because a patient was murdered. She desperately wanted to go to the police station, but she couldn't. The responsibility to make sure that both Victor and her mother weren't actual suspects of the crime rested on her shoulders. Victor had to be innocent if she wanted to keep the job (it's not like he had the nerve to murder anyone anyway). Her mother, well, she wouldn't be able to handle herself in jail. She couldn't have done it. It was impossible. But a strong case could be made against her. She was the mistress. Clara craved for more details of the case and had plenty of time to get to the office, so she read the newspaper article.

Several old and new items of information emerged in the opening paragraph. Mitch was found in the entryway of his estate. He had just arrived when he fell because he still had his black peacoat and sunglasses on. It was most likely a quick, painless death and he most likely died while erect, before hitting the floor. The time of death is estimated to be 11:30 AM (just one half hour after he left the office). He was found only a few minutes later. There were several items of evidence obtained from the body that the police would not disclose at the time. A statement from primary detective Ed Pearson read:

"We are greatly affected by the loss of Mitch Greenway. He was an incredible philanthropist and contributed much to the Houston community. We can safely say the cause of death was some form of poisoning, although we await the coroner's report for more specific information. We do not believe it was unintentional. Yes, he was murdered. Several physical factors and pieces of evidence indicate this suspicion. We are pursuing several paths that may lead to the culprit."

It was going to be an uphill battle. There were several key pieces of information Clara needed in order to narrow the field of suspects. First and foremost would be what type of poison it was, which would soon be confirmed by the coroner. When would the body be inspected, anyway? Would she have access to that information? Additionally, she wanted to know what "pieces of evidence" were found on Greenway. They sounded concerning.

Clara finished her cereal, put the bowl in the dishwasher, and went over to check the fireplace for the third time since last night. Her mother wanted to burn the tickets despite their online footprint and record with the airline. Clara said she would, but threw a few blank papers in the fire instead. They couldn't get away from her—they were important. The tickets were under another name, anyway, so if they were out of her possession, she would never be caught. Clara had asked her mother if there was anything else—hotel reservations, car rentals, anything. Her mother handed over fake IDs and passports that matched the names on the tickets and even a credit card.

After confirming there was nothing but ashes above the wood (her mother needed to be convinced they were gone), Clara grabbed her keys and went straight to the car. To her surprise, it had finally warmed up to usual temperatures in the city. It was almost sunny, and certainly warm. Her jacket flew to the backseat, and she drove back to the office, or the probable crime scene.

Victor wasn't in yet when Clara arrived. Maybe he thought it looked strange if he was still sleeping there. He probably booked a hotel because it was hard to imagine his wife took him back already. Clara opened the door and the wave of warmth hit her. She had forgotten to turn the heat off the day before and now it was certainly unnecessary. She threw her purse on the desk and switched on the lights. A strange sensation of disappointment flushed through her. The excitement was over, and it was back to work. It couldn't have been over, though. It had only just begun. She would lead the police to the deserving criminal and be thanked by everyone. Maybe she would get a medal for her detective skills. Oh, was she kidding? Of course she wouldn't get a medal. If anything, she would seem *suspicious* by getting involved in the case. She just needed to protect the innocent.

There were eight new messages on the phone. Every single one of Victor's patients for the day cancelled. It was bizarre—the newspaper never even mentioned his name. Clara booted up the computer to see if there were any other stories that could have introduced him. The results were not good. Multiple articles.

One title read, "The Doctor's Orders: Did a deranged psychiatrist poison Mitch Greenway?" It went on to reveal that Mitch had an appointment with Victor Weihen the morning of his death. One witness, Mrs. Whittle, said, "He did look very tense. He was wearing sunglasses, holding some papers. He was not relaxed whatsoever." Why would she say something like that? She had been going to Victor for years. This would ruin his career… and hers. She needed to realign her approach— get serious. Perhaps his reputation was still salvageable. The police had said nothing in the article, it was all merely speculation. Still, no one was showing up for their appointment. She had her chance to conduct a real investigation. She meticulously scanned through the resources of the internet, but nothing about the affair came out. Thank the devil.

She began to pack up her things; obviously, there was no reason to be there if the patients weren't going to arrive. As she began her way out, though, Victor was just coming through the door.

"Clara," he looked nervous, sleepless, and dirty. "What are you doing?"

"Oh, Victor, I…" She bit her lip and took a step back. There was a very real possibility that he was a killer. It was surreal. "I was leaving because, well, all of your patients cancelled. You should probably go home, too."

There was no look of surprise on his face. He was sad and completely expecting the cancellations. He chose not to leave and asked her to stay. Of course. It's not like she had to save his reputation or her mother's innocence or anything. It's not like she was at risk of losing her job and quite possibly needed to compile a resume. Sometimes he just got on her nerves a little too much. She had a plan, and he was just beginning to ruin it. As always, everything went his way.

He waddled over to his office, acting as if he was some victim in this situation, which could have been true. Clara still didn't like his attitude, as if he should be in his office while his life broke down completely; there were other priorities. So she made a list of who she needed to talk to and wrote down their numbers on a piece of paper. Miles Greenway was the first person written. He was a prime suspect—the police would soon be after him. Then there was Linda. Did she know about the affair? If she had, it would easy to blame her for revenge, but it was unlikely. And it would be very tricky. She couldn't just go around pointing fingers at anyone. Not everyone was guilty.

Then there were the patients: Leiman Turner—who Clara didn't know much about but was inclined to find out—and Mrs. Whittle, the talkative, manipulative old lady. There was a possibility that she knew a few things because she was a real gossip. It was hard to predict what Clara would get out of her, but she was worth speaking to. Who else? At the time, Clara couldn't think of anyone.

The phone rang. Probably a patient for later in the week ready to cancel. But then the raspy voice came on the line. It was Detective Pearson.

"Is Weihen in? We have just a few more questions."

Clara faltered. She said, "He's in." It couldn't be

good; the stories were directing the police instead of the other way around. They also might have found something else. Would they want to question *her* again? Of course not.

Clara walked into his office and said, "The detectives are coming back. Just a few more questions." She said the last part mockingly.

He looked cold. It wasn't good and he knew that. She didn't want to console him, though. She just wanted to make sure she could leave to perhaps pay a visit to Miles Greenway. Victor agreed she could go, but she lingered slightly to see the detectives when they arrived.

They were in the same outfits as the day before when they came through the door. Pearson still looked like a child in the suit that didn't quite fit him and Suds was wearing a white shirt, black pants, and a tie. Suspenders don't particularly look good on young men, but Suds at least attempted to pull them off. Both of them looked tired and each held one of those gigantic coffee cups from Starbucks that could quench the thirst of an entire nation.

"Oh, good morning!" Clara said. She was too perky, it was weird. "He's in his office."

Pearson was already looking at the office door. He said, "Thank you, Ms.—" He started to look at some papers that were erroneously attached to a clipboard. He forgot her name. Was he kidding? Not that she cared, it was better that way. If he doesn't know her, he doesn't know her mother.

"Tulit. But you can call me Clara." The line came with a big helping of attitude. They didn't even notice as they limped over to Victor's office like zombies. They must have pulled an all-nighter. As Clara walked out, she saw a glimpse of something in Suds' hands. It was what looked like a pile of papers in a plastic bag marked, "EVIDENCE." It was rather curious. What could they have been? Clara brushed it off, though, and drove home.

She hesitated in deciding what to do next. Interview witnesses, suspects; it was the only logical thing to do. But she needed a plan as to how to go about it. When she rounded the corner onto her street, luck struck her. In front of the house was a black Mercedes. A Greenway.

Two Greenways, actually. Miles and Linda were sitting in the living room of the house when Clara walked in. They were on the couch along with her mother. Tracy was in the chair closest to the television.

She wanted to ask the Greenways questions, but alone. She didn't want her mother or sister to be anywhere near them. Mom had such a loud mouth, who knew what would slip out? It was strange the Greenways were there at all. Mitch and mom were the real friends in this family-acquaintance crap. Clara assumed the whole connection would just dissolve after he died.

"Hello!" Clara said. It was wildly inappropriate, what was she thinking? Mitch was just murdered and she said hello as if nothing was wrong. Linda looked up. She was unmistakably crying before Clara had come in. Miles smiled.

Clara had to save herself. She said, "Miles." She faked an upsetting face. "Linda," she said, turning her

head as if she couldn't even bear all the tragedy. "I'm—"
She paused. Perfect timing. She looked down. "I'm so
sorry for this obscene loss."

Linda said, "Thank you, Clara. That means so
much." Clara sat down. She thought about what answers
she wanted out of them. Where were they at the time he
died? Who found Mitch's body? What was on the body
(if they knew)? Any recent arguments? How was she
going to get this information out of them at this awkward
little family encounter? Just try to be nice.

It must have been quite obvious that she was still
confused as to why they were in her living room because
her mom said, "I invited the Greenways over. I supposed
they needed some friendly support through these hard
times." She gave a glance to Linda, who smiled in return.
Her mom was a complete bitch. What mistress gives the
widow of her dead secret lover friendly support? Even
Tracy winced.

Clara said, "So thoughtful of you. How are you
holding up?"

Miles decided to answer. He said, "It's been hard,
Clara. I mean, what is one supposed to do? Sure, family
members die all the time. But my dad was murdered.
Someone decided that their ambitions or gains were
more important than his life. Brutal. Heartless." He
started to mutter random words like that.

Clara took a chance and asked, "Were you the one
to—you know—*find* him?" She immediately regretted
jumping in too soon. Her mom gave one of those *stop it,
you're rude* looks, but the damage was already done. At
least it would yield an answer.

Miles recovered from the "awful" question and said, "Yes. I was the one." His eyes focused on something in the room, but clearly his thoughts weren't there. It was important to note that there were no tears in Miles' eyes at any point. "He had called me on his way back from the doctor, where you work," he looked at Clara, "just to tell me he was coming home. I offered to go out and do something with him. He was always bummed after being with the doctor. I'm not sure why. I thought we could go for a game of golf or something. I drove over to my parents' estate and waited for him.

"Then, after a little while, really, I heard the front door shut. I knew he was home. I thought for sure he would come upstairs to the billiards room, so I waited. About ten minutes later, I ran downstairs to see what he was doing. He was on the ground, lifeless, still in his coat. I ran to him, shook him, but he was gone. I called the police immediately."

He was lying. His face gave him away. There was something not right about his story. Clara couldn't pinpoint it. He told it with very little emotion, too. Miles was a prime suspect at this point.

Clara asked, "Did he have anything with him?" Everyone looked at her again. She didn't squirm, but tried to look caring. As if the question would help him with his sorrow.

"Uh, I don't know, Clara. He had his jacket, that's really all I saw."

"No papers?"

"What? No. Is there something that I don't know?"

He was acting defensively. She needed to abort the

hard-pressing questions. She said, "No, I was just in the office today, and the detectives came by—Pearson and um, Suds—and they were carrying this evidence bag with a pile of papers."

He said, "I didn't see any papers. Why were the detectives there? Something to do with Weihen?"

He didn't know that Weihen was a suspect; he hadn't gotten that far. She shouldn't have said anything. She couldn't have people thinking that Victor did it. She lied. "They just wanted to ask him a few questions because he saw Mitch that day. They asked me a few, too." Her throat was drying up.

"Oh. That makes sense," he said. He gave a slight look to Tracy but she remained passive.

Linda crossed and uncrossed her legs. Something was on her mind. Sure enough, she said, "Dear, you're forgetting what the police told us."

Clara said, "The police? What did they say?" She sounded much too excited. It wasn't her best day, admittedly.

Miles and Linda looked at each other, momentarily deciding who would reveal the new information. Miles gave an unusual glance to his mother and she looked ashamed.

"Maybe we shouldn't," Miles said.

"You're right. I'm sorry, it really doesn't matter." Linda gave an apologetic look to Clara and then her mom. Clara's hopes dissipated. What weren't they saying?

Clara tried to laugh casually and said, "If it doesn't matter, then you should just say it. Act like it doesn't matter." Everyone squirmed. The tension in the room was like a weight pulling down on Clara. Miles looked nervous and Linda gently threw up her arms.

Linda said, "Well, there was a small stick of lipstick in Mitch's coat pocket. They asked me if I could identify it as mine, and I told them I couldn't. It was unused, wrapped in its original packaging. I suppose Mitch bought it for me as a thoughtful little gift." She gave a little grin. Miles winced a tad.

Clara tried to look like nothing was going through my mind, but she shot her mom a quick glance, nevertheless. Her mom was touching her face near her lips, looking out the window. She didn't make eye contact with Clara. She knew the lipstick wasn't for Linda.

Clara announced that she needed to go upstairs for a minute, and like magic, Miles and Linda mentioned they should "really be getting home now anyway." They both stood up. Linda began the usual process of kissing everyone's cheeks. Miles hugged Tracy and then shook Clara's hand. He gave a kiss to her mom. After multiple sorrowful goodbyes, they were finally out the door and into the shiny little Mercedes.

Watching it drive away, Clara thought about Miles and his story. Much of it did not add up. He said he wanted to go golfing with his father, but the course at the country club was closed on Mondays. She knew that because Mitch had always complained that Mondays were course maintenance days. Miles mentioned he knew his father was dead before even coming close to the body for examination. For some reason, she did not believe he had a conversation with his dad on the phone that morning. But that could be easily verified. The strangest, most bizarre thing about Miles Greenway, however, was that he didn't seem to show a hint of surprise or even emotion when he found his father's cold, lifeless body. Or he just left that part out. And he was not the one to call the police. That was Linda.

Chapter Six

The next thing to do was to get the other key witnesses to talk. Miles seemed like he was not going to give away much more, and most of the things he said were probably lies. Clara had the rest of the day off. Pearson and his partner were speaking to Victor and she would have to find out what that was about later. For now, she just needed to see the other suspects and figure out what angles she could further explore.

She perused the list—names, numbers, and addresses—and found the person who lived the closest to her was Mrs. Whittle. In fact, they only lived two minutes from each other. Whittle lived in an apartment building on Dunlavy. Clara must have passed by it a million times. It was new construction, but seemed to look either cheap or stale. Not particularly the best place, but there was worse. Clara decided to give her a call.

"Ms. Tulit, how are you? Is there something wrong with my appointment?" she asked.

She was probably the only patient who actually kept her appointment at that point. Clara said, "No, no, Mrs. Whittle. I actually wanted to talk to you. Um, about Mitch Greenway."

There was a pause. "I don't know anything about Mitch Greenway, Ms. Tulit."

"I know you don't know much about him. My memory is just a little hazy." Clara raised her hand to her head to be authentic. "Maybe if I could hear about what you saw yesterday, things will clear up for me."

Another silence. She wasn't saying anything, so Clara continued, "You see, the police think that it might have been Victor—Dr. Weihen. I think we both know it wasn't him; he wouldn't hurt anyone. It's quite important we do figure out *who* it was, though. The police, well, they don't know Victor. We do. Understand? We could help them take a different route for their investigation."

Her voice was a bit higher and coarse when she said, "Dr. Weihen? He would never do such a thing. Then again, I don't know him too well…"

"Oh, Mrs. Whittle! You've been seeing him for years!" Clara cried. She remembered scanning Whittle's record in the system. The old lady had started seeing him in May of 2012.

After a short silence and what sounded like an exaggerated sigh, Whittle said, "Very well. I suppose we could compare stories. The police haven't even come to see me yet. I should think they never will."

Clara didn't say that maybe she could go down to the police department to testify. The time would come for her to suggest that. For now, she needed to secure the meeting. She asked, "May I come 'round to your home? You're on Dunlavy, correct?"

"That's right, Ms. Tulit. You may come in an hour. It must be brief, though. I'm expecting guests at four. That means you'll need to leave by two thirty so I can prepare. If you come in an hour by one thirty, that gives us an hour. Does that make sense?"

"Yes. I'll see you at one thirty. Thank you, Mrs. Whittle."

She hung up.

Clara had an hour to sort out what she would say to Whittle. She just wanted to know what the woman saw, if she had any suspicions, and that's it. If there was anything Clara could glean from their conversation, so be it. But she hoped that really nothing would come out. Unless, of course, it pointed in another direction from her mother or Victor. She still hoped that her job would be preserved after all this. It wasn't selfish, just a desire.

This was a perfect time to involve her sister. Clara told her she could help in the investigation, and getting information from harmless witnesses would be the best possible way. Tracy was an avid murder mystery fan. She could think creatively—she was good at predicting the outcomes of the stories she immersed herself in. All of those ridiculous plots had situations that would never happen in real life, so Clara knew she would never arrive at the truth. But perhaps she could present ideas and help inspire. Clara needed to rattle her thoughts to someone, anyway.

She went upstairs and knocked on Tracy's door. It was funny—she usually knocked, but never waited for a response and just barged right in. It was an old habit. When she opened the door, she found her sister sitting in front of the vanity table. Tracy was humming and smiling in the mirror before she noticed Clara and turned around.

"Clara! Can you believe this whole thing with mom? I have no idea how she possibly could have had the nerve to have an affair with a married man! Mitch Greenway, no less." She was enjoying herself, talking like it was gossip. Her tone sounded concerned, but her eyes gave her excitement away. "Do you think... do you think the police will find out?"

Clara broke her bubble of fantasy because she needed her to snap out of it. The police clearly weren't going to figure it out. They couldn't find out. "No, absolutely not, Tracy." Clara hopped up on the bed. "Not if *we* have anything to do with it." She needed to intrigue her sister or she would get bored. Tracy was like that.

"What do you mean?" Tracy started brushing her hair. It was clear she was doing it before Clara had knocked on the door, as well.

"Tracy." Clara cleared her throat a little. "I have a few things I need to protect. That *we* need to protect. Mom is a suspicious time bomb. No one knows about her now, but if anything—and I mean *anything*—were to get out, she would surely be the person held responsible. Now I don't think anything will leak... but that leads me to the second thing I need to protect. The prime suspect—the actual suspect with a very real possibility of being convicted—is Victor Weihen, my employer. Greenway was poisoned, as you know. Weihen was the only person to have been known to give something that Mitch could have consumed. Pills." Clara grinned. She couldn't help it. Tracy was now totally into it.

Tracy whipped her head around and lightly threw the hairbrush to the back of the table, causing it to gently hit the mirror. She looked at Clara for a moment, gathering her words. "You're right! Poor Weihen! But you, you can't lose your job. You love that job." She really knew very little.

"Exactly!" Clara lied. Her sister was right about wanting to keep the job. Clara didn't love it, but it certainly gave a paycheck.

Tracy said her next words slowly as if she were trying to clarify the situation. "So we need to simultaneously prove that Victor Weihen is not guilty and hide all information about mom's affair. That's obvious. This is perfect—a real murder mystery. There is the person who it all points towards, but clearly did not do it because it is too obvious. That's Weihen. There's the person who has too many secrets, but also did not do it because the sleuth thinks that it was probably them. The sleuth needs to be surprised, you see. Then there is the killer! When it is all revealed, it just makes sense. We'll find out, and it will make sense!"

"Precisely," Clara said. Maybe Tracy would be more help than originally anticipated.

"First, we need a list of witnesses."

"I have that."

"Great. Write it down because we need to interview them."

"I will, and I already scheduled the first interview!"

Tracy was ecstatic. "No way! Who is it? Do you think it could have been him? What's against him? When?"

"Calm down," Clara said. "It's not a him, it's a her. Angela Whittle: a patient of Dr. Weihen. She was present in the waiting room when Greenway was there. She may have seen something… or *done* something, of course. Though I highly doubt that. The interview is in about forty-five minutes." Maybe Mrs. Whittle would not be okay with two people showing up to her home. Clara only asked if *she* could come over, not her sister. But Tracy looked too happy, she couldn't let her down. Whittle would have to deal.

"Fantastic! I need to come up with a list of questions. What do we know about her?"

Clara tried to mirror her enthusiasm, but honestly, it was hard to keep up. "Not much. I think she has OCD, but that's it. I know her address and phone number. I don't know what she does. I assume she's married because she goes by misses."

"Does she have a job?" Tracy asked absentmindedly. She had already begun typing the name into Google on her laptop. Clara didn't answer her question. She just left her searching.

Clara went over to her room and went straight to the bed. She just laid there until it was time to go. She thought about her course of actions and made mental notes. She questioned if she was proceeding with the case correctly. If there was a time to choose between mom and Victor, clearly she would need to choose mom. The job wasn't *that* important, right? Besides, Victor was probably the worst person to be around. She deserved a better boss.

The lipstick was a bigger deal than Clara had previously thought—a loose string that was out of her control. Maybe it meant nothing for the police, but it represented something important. She was convinced it was her mom's lipstick when Linda first mentioned it. In case she would ever get the chance to check the brand of the found lipstick, she memorized the name of the brand that her mother swore by. Her mother wore it every day for at least as long as Clara had been living. It never stayed on—it would get everywhere and she would constantly have to reapply it. Clara remembered seeing its stain on her father's clothes sometimes. On his neck. Her mother once drank coffee out of dad's favorite mug and forgot to wash it. The lipstick plastered on and it never came off. Her father smiled and proudly drank from it. The color was a darkish, brightish red, if that makes any sense. The brand was cheap but tried to make it sound fancy with a French-sounding name: Beauté (hint: it wasn't made in France). The shade: Red Dexterity No. 1. Apparently there were multiple "Red Dexterities."

When it was about ten minutes to one thirty, Clara gathered Tracy and they got in the car. Clara was in her normal work clothes—a skirt, tights, white collared shirt, and slightly casual blazer. Her glasses matched the blazer; she liked that. She wore her hair down so it wouldn't look too manly.

Tracy changed into a ridiculous getup that made her look like one of those TV detectives. Hair in a bun, white shirt, black vest (yes, *vest*), pants, complete with a half-length trench coat. She had a notepad in the pocket! Clara tried not to laugh.

"So what's the approach?" Clara asked, thinking she would get a chuckle out of whatever her sister came up with. She was hoping it would be some good-cop, bad-cop scenario but it seemed like Tracy knew exactly what kind of witness they were interviewing.

"Well, I though about it for a while, but I realized that this Angela Whittle isn't going to know anything important. It'll be nice to hear a different perspective from your story, though." She looked at her notepad, avoiding eye contact. Was she questioning Clara's story?

She continued, "Perhaps we'll find something suspicious that you might have missed. We need to cling to anything if you want Victor innocent. Obviously mom didn't do anything, but you see, I never met this Weihen man. To me, he has the largest motive. But you need your job," she said. The last bit was emphasized as if Clara was being a diva or something. What was this attitude?

They parked on the street across from the apartment building. It was a building entirely of rentals—no one owned any homes there. It was strange that a sixty-five year-old woman didn't own a house, or even an apartment. She *rented* one. It was in a building that looked like it catered to young people, too. Probably cheap, but Clara wasn't sure.

The concierge sent them up. Whittle was on the fourth floor and it was quite a walk from the elevator to her place. There was no doorbell, so the two sisters knocked.

A dog barked as Mrs. Whittle opened the door. "Come in, Clara. Oh, now who is this?" Her eyebrows converged. Clara was quick to answer.

"This is my sister, Tracy. She's helping me with my little investigation, Mrs. Whittle. May we come in?"

She said, "Oh, you didn't mention her. Well, Tracy." She emphasized the name because she had just met her, "How do you do?"

"Fine, thank you. We just have a few questions for you, Mrs. Whittle." Tracy looked at Clara and gave her a small nod of approval.

As they walked down the hallway, Mrs. Whittle said, "Investigation? I thought I was just trying to refresh your memory, Clara." She smiled as if she had caught something. She was like that; she practically lived on finding others out.

The apartment was superbly neat. Two bedrooms, but she said she lived alone. The front doorway was on the other end of a hallway that led straight into the living room and kitchen area. In the hallway, there were two doors opposite from one another that led to the bedrooms. They sat down at the small dining table near the windows. The space was small, but not too bad.

There wasn't a speck anywhere. Everything had straight lines that often ended in ninety degree angles with other straight lines. All of the dishes and cups were stacked in the glass cabinets with precision. A large bottle of soap lay next to the faucet and water surrounded the sink. It was obvious she had been washing her hands. Maybe she always does and the water never goes away?

Mrs. Whittle sat down and said, "Well, tell me what you need to know. Remember ladies, we only have an hour. The book club is coming by at four and I need to prepare." She then picked up her tiny dog from the ground, who had sufficiently sniffed the girls' legs and deemed them worthy of being in the home, and placed him on her lap. It was a small white dog; probably a Pomeranian. Then again, Clara was never very good at dog breeds—she never had one.

Tracy froze up a little, she wasn't quite ready. She urged Clara to start talking. She did that sometimes—she would be having fun and all of a sudden quiet down when in company. She expected her big sister to lead the conversation. Clara just took it as a compliment that she was naturally good at communication.

Clara said, "Mrs. Whittle—"

"Please, Clara, we're not at the office. I'm Angela."

"Angela." It was weird saying it. "I guess I'll just start with telling you what I saw. Then you can tell me your experience and we can compare." She gave a nod.

Clara began, "I started my day early because we were just getting back from the holidays, as you know. I opened the office and prepared as usual." She left out that Dr. Weihen was already there, sleeping in his office. Whittle didn't need to know that. It would seem unusual and Weihen didn't need to lose anymore business.

Clara continued, "Then Dr. Weihen came in and started to get ready for the day. He closed the door to his office so I really had no idea what he was doing. He's not a killer, though. I can swear by that! Anyway, the first patient was Leiman Turner. You may not know him. The second was Mitch Greenway and the third was you. No one else came in until much later. Greenway went straight into Weihen's office when he was called. I saw him carrying a strange stack of papers. He left right after. Did you perceive anything differently?"

She straightened her back and looked at Clara with a gaze that seemed like disappointment. She said, "Well, Clara. I seem to remember things quite different from you."

Tracy gave a sharp, inquisitive look. Clara didn't know what to say. She was intrigued herself. "Please tell me what you remember."

"It seems you forgot that Dr. Weihen had spent the night in the office." *Of course* she knew. In Clara's mind, there was a sigh of relief. Whittle gave that look as if Clara were caught again. "I know because he told me. He said he was having problems with his wife. These psychiatry appointments go two ways if you're like me, you know. I ask about his problems too. Next, you entirely forgot to mention the delivery man. He was just leaving as I arrived. He was in Weihen's office *with* Mitch Greenway! And the door was closed, I might add."

The delivery man! What was his name? Danny. She was a genius. If Clara could somehow find out how to make him seem suspicious, the job would be done! Who knew what he was doing with the door closed in Weihen's office?

"You're right!" Clara said. "I genuinely forgot about the delivery man!"

Whittle closed her lips and looked at Clara, her eyes following the secretary's body up and down. Then she looked at Tracy. Eventually, she produced a large sigh as if she was ready to just say something.

In a quieter, hushed tone, she said, "Listen girls, I know why you're here. I know why you're doing this little investigation. But first, let me explain myself."

"What do you mean?" Tracy asked.

She disregarded the question and continued, "I like money! What can I say? I always had a way of finding out secrets. I'm very good at that."

Clara felt drops of sweat grow on her back. "Mrs.—Angela, what do you mean?" She was loud, so Whittle snapped out of her little storytelling trance.

Whittle looked confused. "Well, you know." She looked like she was trying to lead a learning child to a logical conclusion. "Your mother's affair."

Tracy and Clara looked at each other, exchanging equally surprised expressions. Clara said, "How do you know about that?" Tracy was looking around, as if paranoid all of a sudden.

She said, "Girls, I don't have time for you to be confused. You came because I have been blackmailing Greenway, correct?"

Clara's mouth dropped. What was she talking about?

"Now, I don't know how you found out, Clara. Clearly the doctor has a looser tongue than I thought. He throws patient confidentiality out the window! Anyway, I made sandwiches. Are you hungry? I am. Then we can really discuss what we want to discuss."

Chapter Seven

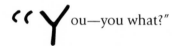ou—you what?"

"They're cucumber, is that alright?" She yelled from the kitchen.

She was so casual, but her words were so serious. It was incomprehensible. It was new weight in Clara's brain. How was this possible? She knew about mom's affair—that means others could have known, too. Clara needed to get to the bottom of it. Whittle mentioned blackmail. What did she mean? Was she blackmailing Greenway because she knew he was seeing Clara's mother?

Clara yelled, "Listen, Angela! Forget the damn sandwiches and come in here. Tell us the meaning behind what you just said." She looked over at Tracy, who looked like she was still recovering. Perhaps it wasn't the best idea to bring her along. She met Clara's gaze and gave her a brief look that said *I don't know what's going on*. Clara didn't know either.

Whittle came in with the sandwiches. They were cucumber and hummus in between slices of white bread. The crusts were cut off. She slammed the plate down on the table and said, "Now, Clara, don't use that tone with me. I'll explain. But I only have forty-five minutes!" She grabbed a cucumber sandwich and started eating it into a napkin.

While she was recounting the whole story, which was thankfully coherent, Clara was going over in her head what to do next. Ask her to tell no one… or *threaten* her? Could she even do that? She wanted to speak to Mrs. Whittle, but she didn't think having Tracy there would be the best idea. She needed to be alone. Just one little question. One answer. That's all she needed.

Anyway, Whittle began her tale. She said, "Now, girls, I don't know how much you know. But I had assumed you knew your mother was having an affair with Mitch Greenway. Your confused reactions, however, have now convinced me otherwise. So, let me tell you: *Your mother has been having an affair with Mitch Greenway.*"

Clara motioned to ask a question but she waved her hand and said, "Now, how do I know? Let's start from the very beginning. It was mid-November, just two months ago. I had my usual Monday appointment, which always came after Mr. Greenway's. I had arrived a bit early and the receptionist (that's you, Clara) was gone from her desk. Well, there was no one in the waiting room, so I called out. No one responded. Now that I think about it, I never even saw you there that day, Clara."

It was true that Clara had taken a sick day sometime in the middle of November. It could have been that Monday. She rarely caught anything but when she did, Victor just kept running the office without a receptionist.

Whittle continued, "Naturally, I intended to go into

the Dr. Weihen's office. Perhaps he would be there alone and we could begin early. That way I would know I wasn't waiting for nothing, you see? But then, as I got closer to the door, I could hear muffled shouting. I have a small tendency to eavesdrop. It's one of my few flaws." She took a bite of the sandwich. She stared at her guests. Clara blinked to let her know she was not going to comment on the arrogant remark.

"When I put my ear up to the door, I could hear crystal clear. A man was speaking to Dr. Weihen. He was speaking passionately, something along the lines of, 'I don't know what to do, Doc. I've been seeing her for maybe a month or two now! Has it gone too far? It's not too serious, but is it unhealthy? I've known her for years. I don't know if I could stop.' And then Dr. Weihen responded, 'Mitch, it's not always the best idea to indulge one's feelings like this, but I don't see how it could do any harm, really. If you love the woman, then just be careful about it.' That's when my ears really perked up! I could tell from the name *Mitch* that it was Mr. Greenway. It made sense; he always went before me. And he was in love with some woman. To me, it didn't seem like it was his wife!"

"What happened next?" Tracy asked, eyes glistening. She was becoming a little too interested in the whole thing.

Whittle finished the small sandwich and looked hesitantly if she should take another. There was no time for her to take five minutes to decide if she wanted a sandwich. She just needed to get back to the story. So Clara was prepared and acted quickly. She picked one up from the plate and handed it to the old lady. Whittle gave some thankful nod that Clara didn't care for. Hurry up, your book club is coming, she thought.

Whittle said, "I listened for more. The information happily streamed into my ears. Greenway said, 'Listen, Doc, let's get one thing straight. I don't *love* her. I *love* Linda. This thing with Carin, it's just a fling.' Then Wei-hen asked, 'Her name is Carin?' And Greenway said, 'Oh, I think I might have said too much. Oh to hell with it. It's not like you can say anything! Clara's not even here, anyway. There's patient confidentiality, right? The person is your receptionist's mother, Carin Tulit. We've known each other since college—we even dated for a time back then. I suppose we rekindled our interest in each other.' Can you believe that? And I was listening to it all!" She took a bite of her sandwich. She grinned as if she was some master puppeteer. The woman was omniscient. Clara looked over at Tracy. Time was of the essence. Whittle would push them out soon.

"How did you start blackmailing him?" Tracy asked. She seemed to have quite a lot of questions, too. She was writing in her pad.

Whittle said, "Let me get to that, Tracy." She looked at Clara and said, "Considering you weren't there, I thought it would be perfectly normal for me to barge right in there and innocently ask if anyone's in the room. So I did just that. The doctor asked if they could just have a few minutes more before we began our session, but I closed the door behind me. Greenway was rich, and now I knew one of his biggest secrets—I wasn't going to lose my chance. I mean, look around girls! This apartment isn't glittering gold. When I divorced, I was left with nothing! Now I work at the fine arts museum for an outrageously low amount of money.

"Anyway, I closed the door behind me and smiled. I said, 'Carin Tulit, Mr. Greenway? Isn't that a bit… risky?' I bit my lip, it felt so good. He absolutely froze as he realized I was listening through the door. Dr. Weihen looked a bit frazzled, too. Greenway said, 'I don't know what you are talking about, Mrs.—' I gave him my name, but he didn't care. I said, 'You don't now? Well, I do. You're having an affair, Mr. Greenway. Poor Mr. Greenway. All the riches in the world, but you still needed more.' I remember smiling. I wasn't even nervous, I was just happy. It was the strangest feeling. The rest of the meeting was like clockwork. Dr. Weihen left the room, as I imagined he would. I sat down and I gave him my offer. Fifty thousand a month, or I tell every living soul in Texas. He reluctantly agreed."

Clara was too angry to hold anything in anymore. She yelled, "Angela! How could you do that to a man like Greenway! I get it, you wanted money. But you're a fool—do you have any idea how dangerous that move could have been! Greenway is a powerful man."

The woman put down her sandwich and closed her eyes. When she opened them, she shifted slightly as if she were dizzy, acting as if the thought had just occurred to her. Clara had a prominent feeling that it hadn't. Whittle was known to be over the top. She said, "Clara, you know Mr. Greenway. He's a stand-up guy. It's obvious from all the stories about him in the papers. He would never harm an old lady like me."

How could a stand-up guy have an affair? Was she crazy? He was as sleazy as they came. "But you still took advantage of him," Clara said. All of a sudden, the lady disgusted her.

Whittle's grin vanished all too quickly. Her eyes started to water. She said, "It's not fair! I didn't have enough money for December's rent. I was going to have to go somewhere else. There wasn't enough money for anything, really. I most likely would have been on the streets! Did that *occur* to you? That I could have been homeless! Mitch was a billionaire. Fifty thousand is practically what he spends on tips at the country club. What he *spent*." She looked down at the sandwich. "I don't feel very good. Please let yourselves out."

Clara and Tracy stood up. They started walking out and Clara thought about the question. It was now or never. She told Tracy she forgot her phone and started back into the living room while her sister had already gone out the front door. As she got into the living room, Angela Whittle was still on the couch. Clara banged her hand on the table and she opened her eyes. In a hushed voice, Clara said curtly, "Dr. Weihen knew about this affair. Who else knows?"

She looked up with puffy eyes. "No one. No one. I didn't tell a soul. I stayed true to my word for the deal—I'm not that stupid."

"Did the doctor tell anyone?"

"No."

"How do you know?"

"He didn't want to be involved. He told me during our session right after. He said it was wrong what I did."

It was one of those rare occasions that Clara agreed with Victor. She didn't ask anything else as she dashed out. She dug her phone out of her purse to show her sister that she had retrieved it. As she closed the front door to apartment 4125 on Dunlavy, Clara couldn't help but think that Mrs. Whittle could have killed Mitch Greenway.

* * *

They were out the door of the building and about to cross the street when Tracy gave her one of those looks she always gave. Like a lost puppy, pleading for someone to save her. As always, she expected her sister to step up to the challenge.

They crossed and Clara said, "Don't worry, Tracy."

"She knows about mom."

"That doesn't mean there are other people that know."

"Dr. Weihen knows."

"He's probably forgotten by now." It was an unconvincing lie. "Besides, this is actually a silver lining. Mrs. Whittle knew about the affair. She blackmailed Greenway for money. Then Greenway died. Why? Well, a perfectly plausible solution is he decided to stop sending money and Whittle wouldn't stand for it!"

Tracy nodded, trying to take in the facts. Her demeanor changed; the light in her eyes reappeared. The sleuth in her was crawling back out. She looked like she was putting facts together.

"Revenge!" she said, as if agreeing with Clara. "It's true—the blackmail artist wouldn't simply reveal the secret. If she did that, she would absolutely *never* see any money again because she wouldn't have the upper hand anymore."

Clara must have forgotten about Tracy's intelligence. She brought her sister along so that she would feel involved in something, but she was actually proving to be functional. It was a smart move. Clara inquired, "But why would she kill him? Certainly, that would stop the flow of money altogether."

"You're right, it would. From *him*. There are more people she can blackmail with the secret, though! Telling Linda about it would be risky, of course, because she was his wife. She might not want to keep it secret if she knew. The two people that would be strategic for her to tell the secret to and have them pay her to keep quiet would be our own mother and Miles Greenway."

"Miles Greenway?"

"He would want to protect his mother from betrayal and embarrassment."

Tracy made some interesting points. Though, Whittle would never go after mom now because she knew they would stop it. They were the only ones who were aware of her knowledge about the affair. They were the only ones who knew she was a true suspect, and that she could have killed Greenway. But Miles, well, it would be easy for her to blackmail him. He's young, so she probably considers him stupid as well. He would want to save his mother from any emotional pain and protect his father's reputation, so maybe he buys Whittle out. It would make an enormous amount of sense! Clara felt a rush. She wanted to see Miles Greenway again. Alone or with Tracy. They needed to learn if Whittle had already gotten to him.

They arrived home and Clara mapped out the next twenty-four hours. Miles was especially promising, but they had to wait. There were still other suspects. She walked through the door and went straight upstairs into her room. She told Tracy to stay close because they would be going out later.

She wanted to contact Leiman Turner. She didn't know enough about him, so she wanted to learn more. Whittle seemed suspicious and dangerous, but she needed to be absolutely exact when it came time to decide the killer. Eventually, she would have to present her entire case to Pearson and Suds, and they would ask questions. No stone could be left unturned.

Leman Turner had to be seen that day. The next day, in the afternoon, would be Miles. They had to give Whittle a sufficient amount of time to contact him if she hadn't done so already. It was absolutely essential that he tell them everything. No lies. If she started blackmailing him, Clara would be certain she is the killer.

In the morning, however, she needed to go to work. There was one more person that was vital to the case and could lead to the solution. He made deliveries on Mondays, Wednesdays, and Fridays. Tomorrow was Wednesday, and Clara needed to sneak a word with Danny, the delivery man.

Clara took out the small daily planner she had bought at the office store down on West Gray. It hadn't been used until she started to scribble the contact information for all of the witnesses on it. The first page held all the phone numbers and addresses stolen from the office's files. Leiman Turner was second on the list, just below Angela Whittle. He lived farther than Whittle, but not much of a distance. He was in Bellaire, which was maybe twenty minutes away, assuming there was light traffic, of course. There was always traffic.

Clara brought out her cell phone and hesitated a moment to dial the number. It was a bit strange that she was calling one of Victor's random patients at home from her cell. It was worth it, though. He would understand. Or would he? Maybe he would find it a bit too unusual that a doctor's secretary, who really had no place wedging herself into a murder case and playing investigator, was interviewing witnesses and suspects without the law's permission. The risk was worth the payoff. This was no longer about Clara's job. It was about her family.

On the third try, she finally unlocked her iPhone. She clicked on the little green icon and plugged in the numbers. When she heard the first ring, her muscles tensed. She was already kicking herself because she was unready. She needed the right words. Her brain turned to sludge and she could't think of anything to say. He picked up.

"Hello?" There was a pause. A little louder, he said again, "Hello?"

She knew what was happening, and knew she needed to say something. A grunt came out of her mouth, and then she snapped into the conversation. "Hi, hello, sir. This is Clara Tulit, from Dr. Weihen's office. Is this Leiman Turner?"

"No, this is his wife." Clara swallowed her spit. His wife had the manliest voice of any *man* she knew. She wasn't too familiar with Leiman's own voice, so she had just assumed it was him. It took a long time for her to come up with a response.

"Oh—"

"I'll get him for you," she said. The woman shouted for Leiman and after about twenty seconds, he spoke into the phone.

"Who is this?"

"This is Clara Tulit, from Dr. Weihen's office."

"Hello, Ms. Tulit. I've been meaning to call. I don't think I will be continuing under Dr. Weihen's care."

Clara shrugged. "Oh, that's all right. Don't worry, no one is." She cringed—that wasn't very professional. It was meant as a joke, but Clara sensed he didn't smile. "*I* wanted to talk to you, actually. You were at the office yesterday morning. Your appointment was just before that of Mitch Greenway, who, as you may know, died soon after. The police think this death is in connection with his visit to Dr. Weihen's office. They think that Dr. Weihen was perhaps the perpetrator. Now, you may have your doubts, but I *know* Victor Weihen did not commit this crime. I was wondering if we could meet and discuss what you saw. I was there, of course, but I don't have the best memory. I just want to compare our perspectives, you see. Make sure that I'm aware of everything that happened."

There was a slight break, then a sound of muffled speech. He had clearly covered the microphone and was speaking to someone else. He said, "Okay, Ms. Tulit. I don't agree with you about Weihen, but I suppose we could talk. It's not like I have anything else to do. Where do you live?"

"Oh, um," She didn't want to give an exact address. "In the museum district. I'll be with my sister for the rest of the afternoon… if that's fine with you."

"Okay, meet me at the Starbucks on Shepherd at three thirty."

Chapter Eight

It was the fifteenth of December that Clara learned of her mom's grand relationship plans with Mitch. It was evident that they had seen each other quite a few times since the night at the house. Mom was always going to "book club." She even pretended to read books to make the lie feel more genuine. It was easy to see right through it because the club would meet at sporadic times during the month. Most book clubs didn't meet more than once a month—let alone more than once a *week*. She insisted the group was comprised of fast readers. The week before, she was carrying a book out the door, presumably for Tracy and Clara to see the authenticity of the club, and Clara spoke up.

She asked, "What book did you read this half-week?" It came off as sarcastic.

"Oh," she fumbled with the book and read the title right from the cover. She didn't even memorize the name. "It's this wonderful little novel called *The Faded Sun*."

"I've never heard of it," Clara said, looking at her nails. She didn't know quite what she was doing. There was nothing to gain. But she was having fun trying to catch her mother in the lie.

"It's new." Then her mother grabbed the door handle and rushed out.

But on the fifteenth of December, Clara decided to follow her.

"I'm going to book club. You girls go get dinner, okay?" She was looking at her watch. She didn't bother with an actual book this time. Clara had just come in from turning on the Christmas lights for the night. The house always looked the best around the holidays. They lined the brick structure with white lights—the warm yellow-white lights, not the white-white lights that looked tacky.

Clara quickly took the plunge and covered for her soon-to-be absence. She said, "Oh, looks like Tracy will be alone. I have to leave in a few minutes. Laurie invited me for a drink." She studied her mom's face.

"Laurie Kimball?"

"Yep, that's right." She was an old high school friend. Clara went out with her every so often. The last time they saw each other was over the summer. Naturally, there was no intention of seeing her that night, but it was a golden excuse.

"Very well. Get some food, Tracy. I'll leave some money." She always left money for Tracy because she had no job. She expected Clara to pay for her when they went out. Clara didn't mind, but it was a little rude to make her pay *every* time.

She left the house and all of a sudden, Clara was in a scramble. She grabbed her keys and purse, put on a used sweater that rested on the table by the door, quickly hollered to Tracy, and made her way out. Mom was already backing out of the driveway when she jumped into her car. She slowed down, though, because she needed to keep her distance.

When she saw her mom round the corner, she backed out and sped to the intersection, carefully looking which way her mother went. Clara followed her at a safe distance until they both reached the destination. Clara stayed in her car, headlights off, to watch her mother's next few movements.

The place was a sketchy bar, appropriately named "Wheezy's." It looked like a dump, but it was the perfect place for the two lovebirds to meet up. No one but dead-beats would be there, so Mitch was safe. Mom was also in the clear, as Tracy and Clara would never think to go there.

Clara saw her mother get out of her car and go inside. She was much too dressed up for the place. After she went in, Clara parked on a residential street a few blocks down. She looked in the mirror of her car and desperately hoped she could change her appearance enough for her mother not to notice her. She wouldn't, though. If people don't expect a certain person to be there, they rarely notice that person. But Clara went into her purse and found some cheap mascara, anyway. She painted some under her eyes and laughed. It was so dark, she looked gothic (if that is the correct terminology). She pulled back her hair and put it in a net that she had ordered off the internet. The final touch: a blond wig. She was a dark brunette, so her mom would never recognize her. She put it on over the net and tugged it into place. She didn't look too bad as a blond. The eyebrows didn't match, but she wasn't going to make a fuss.

Clara might have been overdressed, too, and although it was okay for her mom, it wasn't for her. She kicked off her high heels and put on the pair of flats that were always in the trunk. She yanked off her silver necklace, too. The sweater covered the dress just enough.

When she walked in, the odor of cigarettes and something that can only be described as "stale" hit her nose. No one was behind the bar, but then again, no one was at the bar. There were several booths lining the walls on either side. On one side, there was a man in sunglasses who looked asleep. Another one, with a beer in hand and a smoke in his mouth, was throwing darts at a crappy target on the wall. He momentarily stopped to look at Clara. She threw on sunglasses that she fished for in her purse and headed to the opposite side. Mitch and her mom were in the farthest booth down. Mitch was in the seat facing Clara, but he wasn't looking up. Mom was presumably sitting across from him facing the opposite direction. Clara quickly walked over and sat in the booth next to them, directly behind her mother and facing away from Mitch. The cushioned backs were so thin, she could feel when her mom bounced on her side of the structure. She started to catch snippets of their conversation.

"I worry about Miles, though," Mitch said. There was a pause. He was most likely sipping the champagne Clara saw him drinking when she walked in.

"Don't. He's a fine young man."

"No, I know he seems well. He just... I don't know if he could run the company very efficiently, you know? He doesn't have that sense of reality. I don't know if that's the right word..."

Mom said, "You mean he's not calculating. He doesn't think ahead."

"Exactly, Carin. Sometimes, you just need to do things you don't want to do. Some of them immoral. The dirty work. I don't think he's cut out for it."

"Ya wanna drink?"

Clara looked up. She was in an intense concentration, focusing on their conversation when she saw a fat, sweaty woman with a pad in front of her.

"What?" she asked.

"A drink? Maybe a burger? We got a special going—uhh." The lady looked at her pad. "Two beers and a burger. Seven ninety-nine. Not bad."

"Do you have a whisky?"

She widened her eyes in one of those nasty, sarcastic ways. "Yeah. Ice?"

"Please." It took the woman probably a full twenty seconds to turn around and walk away. At that point, Clara thought for sure Mitch and mom were going to notice her. But they didn't. She tuned in once more.

"Mitch, it's time," mom said.

"Carin, don't do this now. You know I can't."

"Mitch." She sounded like she was choking up. "I'm giving you an ultimatum."

"Jesus, Carin, what are you talking about?"

She said, "I want to buy tickets—plane tickets—to leave. To pack up and go. After the holidays, of course, in the middle of January. If you don't break it off with Linda and come with me, we are through. And I don't care *who* I tell!" Her body trembled through the cheap booth material. Her voice was getting louder.

There was a small interruption. This would be the end of it. He would say no, and they would part their ways.

"Alright," he said. "I'll do it, but after the holidays."

"You will?"

"Yes, my dear," he said. It was entirely unconvincing. They sat like that, presumably just staring at each other, for the next twenty minutes. Clara had her whisky. She couldn't help but think what a huge mess this would become if Mitch tried to leave Linda.

Mom got up to go to the bathroom, so Clara took her chance to leave. Everything was wrapped up there— they were going to try to go on a new adventure. But as she was leaving, she heard Mitch Greenway make a phone call.

***

Tracy and Clara got in the car once again. Clara was a little nervous this time around. She didn't know what Leiman Turner would say. She barely even *knew* Leiman Turner. She just knew he was in the office that day. Therefore, he could have killed Mitch. Clara had told Tracy a little earlier that they were meeting him and her tech savvy sister did a search for him. She found his Facebook page fairly easily, Clara was told.

As they pulled out of the driveway and started down the path of the surreal-looking trees, Tracy said, "Now, I don't know much. But here's the info I have." She was reading off her tiny little notepad. "Turner is forty-five. He has a wife named Lena and a kid named Peter, who is fifteen and goes to that nice Bellaire public school."

She had figured out a lot just from a social media account. Clara's fingers were tightening around the steering wheel as they drove past a fast food restaurant she vomited in when she was five.

"But get this," Tracy continued. "He's some kind of scientist. He works for a company called 'Ashburn Chemicals.' You know what they do?" Her eyes glistened as they wandered the pad once more. "Produce chemicals for multiple purposes. They sell to pharmaceutical companies, manufacturing plants, private laboratories, and even schools and universities."

"A chemical company?" Clara asked. "You're not saying—"

"I'm not saying anything! But if I were saying anything, I would mention that he has access to quite a lot of toxins. Mitch was murdered by poison, wasn't he?"

Clara swallowed the lump that was forming in her mouth and down her throat. She attempted to change lanes, but noticed there was a car in her blind spot at the last second. The car beeped its horn and she swerved back, just passing a red light as she returned her gaze to the front.

"Are you okay?" Tracy asked.

"What? Yeah, I'm fine. Did you see that woman? She was talking on her cell phone, not even paying attention. Stuff like that should be illegal like it is in other states. Too many crazy drivers."

Tracy didn't respond presumably because Clara was obviously covering for her mistake by blaming someone else. It was a rather odd error because she was a good driver. She thought about how Leiman Turner was a chemist, though. He went into Weihen's office before Mitch. Could it be possible that he slipped something into one of the pill bottle samples? Surely, Victor wouldn't have such a thing lying around. Did Victor ask Turner to bring a toxin for him? Was this a joint operation? There wasn't a motive for Leiman Turner to kill Mitch. Yet.

They pulled into the Starbucks parking lot. The drive-thru lane was busy with eight cars in the line. Hopefully, it wasn't crowded inside the store.

"A mocha frappuccino with extra chocolate sauce on the whipped cream. What's that? Oh, *venti*." Tracy ordered first. Clara looked around the store and saw no sign of Leiman Turner. She scouted a few tables, though. There was one open in the corner and she told Tracy to go take it. She'd wait for the drinks.

"Yeah, I'll take a grande black tea lemonade. No classic syrup please." Clara knew the Starbucks lingo—she was practically addicted to their iced tea. She paid, grabbed the drinks, and plopped down opposite Tracy, who had pulled a third chair to the table.

A few minutes later, Turner entered the store. He was in a light blue, button-down shirt and relaxed pants. They were probably khakis, but not *fancy* khakis. He had his lab coat folded over his arm as if to hide it. He was wearing cheap sunglasses and showed no sign of taking them off. He looked around the store and waved to them when he saw Clara. He held up a finger as if she should wait, and then he stood in line to get a drink. He eventually came to the table with a tall drink. It looked like it was just a regular coffee. Though it had foam coming through the hole in its lid, so maybe it was a cappuccino. A coffee order tells a lot about a person.

"Ms. Tulit. Hello. I have to go to work in about a half an hour. I work late on Tuesdays." He was very curt and looked uncomfortable sitting there. He must have had something to hide.

"Is Ashburn open very late?" Tracy asked.

"I watch over the inventory at night. It's tiring, but it's money. Who are you?"

"I'm Clara's sister, Tracy Tulit. Pleasure to meet you." She put out her hand, which Clara noticed had a diamond ring on the fourth finger. The ring belonged to their mom. She didn't know what Tracy had planned. Clara gave her a questioning stare and she returned it with one of those *I know what I'm doing, you watch* looks. Clara sipped some of her tea.

Tracy continued, "I'm helping Clara with the investigation."

"Investigation? I thought we were just discussing what we remember from yesterday." They really needed to stop using that word.

"You see, Mr. Turner, Mitch Greenway is dead. He's gone from this world, do you understand? Someone is responsible and the detectives think it might be Dr. Weihen. Now, clearly it's not Dr. Weihen—he wouldn't hurt a fly!" Tracy was really schmoozing it up. It was like watching a one-woman act.

"Listen, let me just make it easy and tell you what I know. I'll admit I've made some questionable decisions."

Clara squeezed Tracy's hand under the table stop

whatever act she was doing, whatever angle she thought she was taking. He was getting to the good stuff. "Okay, tell us what you know."

"Well, as you know, I came in alone. I assumed I was the first patient. I saw absolutely nothing out of the ordinary in the office. I was there for my normal session with Dr. Weihen—"

"And what do you see him for?" inquired Tracy. Clara gave her a stern *that's inappropriate* look. But honesty, she was surprised she wasn't the one who asked it.

"That's private!" He blushed. "Anyway, I came out. I went to you to check out and I saw Greenway in the waiting room. You remember things like that because, you know, he's a billionaire. He was carrying some papers or something. He probably had a lot of work to do."

Clara jumped in, "You saw those papers too?"

"Yeah, why? Is it a big deal?" He checked his watch.

"No, I just—I don't know what they could have been. He never brings document papers like that—he usually has a magazine."

"Well, I don't know anything about that." He hesitated. "After I saw him, I left. And now, I must be getting to work, ladies." He stood up, grabbed his coffee and neatly folded the lab coat over his arm again. So much for an interrogation.

"Hold on, Mr. Turner," Clara said. "You said you made some questionable decisions."

His eyes moved side to side and he glanced at his watch. He sat down and urgently said, "Fine. I'll tell you, but I don't have much time. And let me assure you, I am not a bad person."

"Go on," Tracy said.

"Weihen asked me for a *favor*. At Ashburn, I am in the presence of many chemicals." He sighed. "Long story short, Weihen asked that I provide him with a small amount of a toxin called cifonide. I initially refused but he offered free sessions for life and a rather large amount of money. I accepted only because my son will be trying to go to college in a few years. On Monday, I handed over the supply without asking any questions. Of course I regret it and I'm not even entirely convinced that Weihen used it for... murder." His eyes narrowed and he looked dangerous. "You two cannot tell anyone, you understand?"

In a state of shock, Clara nodded. She could see out of the corner of her eye that Tracy did as well.

"What does cifonide do?" Clara asked.

He said, "I seriously have to go!" In a few seconds, he was out the door.

Tracy said, "I'm just going to use the restroom."

Clara nodded and started to check for emails on her phone. There were about three advertisements from websites that she used years ago. There was also one from Laurie asking to meet up. She had to decline, though, because she never saw Laurie more than once every three months, let alone one. It would look suspicious. She put down the phone. Tracy was taking a while. A whole new line of coffee addicts formed since she left.

Clara looked around and eventually got up and went to the women's bathroom. She knocked—it wasn't locked, so she opened the door. No one was there. Her head started to pulsate. Where was Tracy?

Clara ran out of the bathroom to find her sister rushing in from the front of the store. She ran over to her and gave her a pissed-off *where were you* arm wave.

She was smiling, almost laughing. "Don't worry, Clara, I think Leiman is innocent." She was wiping around her mouth, as if she had smudged her lipstick.

"What happened?" Clara asked.

"Well, you never really let me try my act during our encounter with Turner. After the bombshell of information he dropped on us, I knew you would think he was guilty. He could have lied about giving it to Weihen and just poisoned Greenway himself, right? Well, I wanted to test if he was being honest or if he was a criminal. It's always done in the books!"

"What did you do?"

"As you could tell from the ring, I pretended to be a married woman. But that didn't matter because he was a married man. Anyway, I rushed out of the parking lot and yelled, 'Leiman!' and without hesitating, I gave him the most passionate kiss I've ever given!"

"What?" Now, Clara really couldn't comprehend.

"But he turned away, Clara. He shrugged me off and got angry. He said, 'Don't ever come near me again. Tell that to Clara too.'" She always did the same voice in every one of her imitations.

"But why did you do it?"

"*It's all in the books*, Clara. A man who will cheat would certainly commit a crime. But a man who doesn't cheat—who stays loyal—is always innocent. It's the rules of murder."

Clara raised her eyebrows.

"You're an idiot," she said. Clara walked back to the car, ignoring Tracy's shenanigans. She was preoccupied with her own personal victory. The microphone she wore behind her shirt never felt more comfortable than it did just then.

Chapter Nine

*I*t was early the following day when Clara poured her cereal and prepared for work. She still clung to the hope that she maintained a job, but the truth was, it didn't matter if she showed up on time. Weihen would be there—most likely to get away from his wife—but there were no patients or obligations. Only the delivery man would come at some point late in the morning and she wanted to see him.

Reflecting on Tracy's actions at Starbucks, Clara realized they elicited no real danger. She didn't need to speak to Leiman Turner again, so let him be angry. Although, she secretly hoped that she could wrap the whole situation up and the end result would be him. It wouldn't be too hard— he was the supplier of the poison. She cared for him the least. She could keep her job with Dr. Weihen (she was still in denial), and obviously she wasn't planning on having her mother locked up anytime soon.

When she was done with the bowl of manufactured oats, raisins, and sugar, she once again descended the steps of the nice brick house and hopped into the car. The five minute drive to the office felt like it could have been any other day from the past eight months. She could be going to work, where there were no acts of murder and no overbearing obligations. Sure, she didn't like Dr. Weihen and honestly, she really wanted to quit living with her mom and Tracy. But everything was calmer—she had the option of just save money and eventually being able to break free. Now, she was just hoping her job still existed and her mother was *literally* free.

Clara never actually thought about if her mother did it. How would the police find out? How would Clara find out? There was certainly evidence against her, but not more so than Victor. She shook her head. Her mother was innocent and the police weren't after her. They never would be, she thought. They would never know.

Clara got out of the car and saw that the weather had started to change. The week of cold temperatures had begun to warm and she knew that her jacket was already becoming obsolete. She stared at the building that was Victor's small private practice and wondered what her new job would be if she were to get one. Her mind wandered too much; one of her many flaws. She supposed one's mentality began to fall apart when death invaded and freedom was at stake for trusted family members.

Victor's car was there, so Clara knew he was in the office. Despite his presence, though, the door was locked and she had to search for her stupid keys again. When she entered, the office was already alive: lights whirring, heat blasting (although it wasn't necessarily needed), and coffee boiling. Clara walked over to her desk and put her purse down as usual. She placed it underneath the desk, this time—she had to be more protective of her belongings. She could be face to face with a criminal at any point. She paused. It was naïve for her to be defensive, as if she was the center of the entire case. In truth, she was just a secretary that nosed her way into a high-profile murder investigation. Pearson and Suds didn't even know what she was doing. Maybe she gathered enough information to finally tell them that she was conducting her own research. It all depended on when she would see them again. If at all.

Victor popped his head out of his office and his appearance was dreadful. There were huge bags under his eyes and his hair was all over the place. Clara knew from the smell that he hadn't taken a shower since the last time she saw him. The stench was overwhelming, to say the least. It appeared as if he was in new clothes, however. They were part of his stash of "extras" he kept with the blanket in a dirty cabinet behind his desk. Sometimes when she checked her little security camera, she saw him folding them. They were used a few times; never washed.

"Victor," Clara said. "You look awful."

He said, "What? Oh, no…" He was at a loss for words. "To be honest, Clara, the situation seems to be bad for me. The detectives—they're coming back today. They will probably have more grim news. They say they just want the medicine order archives, but I don't know. I've been up all night—after yesterday, well, I just don't know."

What happened yesterday? She had actually seen him—it seemed like the day was an eternity. It was in the morning with Pearson and Suds, before she ran into the Greenways in her living room. After that, she interviewed Mrs. Whittle and later, Leiman Turner with Tracy. She never felt exhausted, though. In fact, she slept somewhat restfully that night.

"What happened yesterday?" Clara asked. She was just saying her thoughts out loud. She genuinely wanted to know because she didn't quite have the whole Weihen situation figured out. She couldn't think of his *motive* for killing Mitch. It wouldn't present itself.

"Well, why don't you come into my office?" His eyes looked around. It could have been paranoia, but obviously there was no one else there. As always, when there were no patients present, it was just the two of them.

"Okay," Clara said. She checked her purse once more but knew it didn't matter. No one was looking or thinking of taking her purse. Maybe she was as insecure as Weihen. She followed him into his office and he looked out again before he closed the door.

The therapy room was a mess. The blanket was unmade over the leather couch; the pillow had weird-looking stains on it. Clara did not inquire about them. His desk was a disarray of papers, and a bottle of pills sat on the small coffee table. It was opened. She wasn't sure, but she thought he might have been taking medication from the supply of samples (meant for patients) and consuming it himself.

"Dr. Weihen, perhaps you should go home to your wife tonight. This is disgusting," she said. There was no empathy in her voice. No pity.

"What's that?" He looked embarrassed. "No, I don't think I can do that."

"And why is that?"

"Now she thinks I'm a murderer." They both

became silent. Clara didn't want to say anything, though it was interesting that he didn't jump to prove he wasn't the culprit. Maybe he felt he didn't have to prove anything.

She didn't want to be there. She was much better just sitting at her desk and trying to figure out the crime. Sometimes that was all a detective needed: some time to reflect. But she sat down on a small wooden chair in the corner. It was a piece of furniture that was sadly never used due to its placement. It had the name of Weihen's university from Germany inscribed on the back.

She flipped her hair, and with slight intrigue, gave the facts to Victor frankly, but not too harshly. He of course didn't know all that she knew, so she needed to inform him of a few things.

"Listen Victor. The police probably think it was you. At least that was my understanding two days ago—the day Mitch was murdered."

"Mitch? Why do you call him Mitch?"

She stopped and lost her train of thought. "Oh, I um… I know him. He's a family friend of mine."

"Ah." As if he didn't know. He sat down behind his desk and connected his hands as he does when he is with a patient. His fingers intertwined.

"But to be honest, there isn't much evidence against you. They only think that you're a possible source of the poison. You gave him some pills that day. But if you just say that you always give him pills—a weekly sample or whatever—you could make a case for yourself."

He stared and said, "Clara, I don't usually give him a prescription. Not that we fill those here, anyway. It would be ridiculous to say I give him a sample every week. Besides, he has never needed medication. Just therapy."

"Then why did you give him a bottle of pills?" The tension in her stomach grew, but she knew to put it away. This couldn't happen here. "What were they for?"

"I can't talk about it, Clara. I can't talk about it."

She was becoming impatient. The only thing she wanted hear him say was that the pills were actually a legitimate medicine. He could at least *try* to protect his innocence. Clearly, he was lazy and did not think ahead. She got up from the chair and started to leave. "Listen, if I don't know everything…" Of course, she already knew; she was absolutely certain those pills were cifonide. "Then I can't help you."

But then something miraculous happened. She knew he wouldn't open up about the pills. Not to her, at least. He mentioned something else that she was entirely unaware of and was utterly shocking.

"Wait! There's one more thing, Clara." He jumped up, but regained his composure. "I don't know who to tell—but there is one piece of information the police will use against me. It is damning—it drives the 'nail into the coffin,' as they say. Mr. Greenway had some papers when he came to the office two days ago. They were his will."

The papers *were* important.

"He wanted to thank me for my years of dedication and service to him. Mr. Greenway suffered from anxiety and minor depression. I had helped him for years. He wanted to show me that he had placed me in his will. After he died, I would accept a sum of five million dollars from his estate. I couldn't believe it at the time. I thought it was a blessing, but it turned out to be a curse. It's a motive, Clara. And I had nothing to do with it!" He looked hopeless as he plopped himself back into the leather chair.

It was *the* motive. The pieces were coming together, and they didn't look good for Weihen. How would he come out of this one? She couldn't help but think that he *was* the killer. She backed out of the office and through the door. She was nearly convinced, but didn't run out in panic or anything. She just leaned herself against the door. She thought she would fall over, but she didn't. He was in the will and that would be the police's argument. It was not for his "years of service," either. Was he kidding? No one could be fooled with that nonsense. This was five million dollars. He must have performed quite the service, and this was his compensation. The final nail, indeed.

Clara mumbled that she had work to do and walked over to her desk knowing that Weihen would be found guilty. It was only a matter of time. She accepted it, but there was still that urge to discover more. There was something inside her that said *I could still help*. Just needed more facts; she wanted to interview more witnesses. Were there even any more? Perhaps she just wanted something to do. Was this just feeding her desire to feel important? No, it was impossible to give up. If she didn't push boundaries and ask questions, no one would ever find out the truth, especially with Pearson and Suds running the show. She took a deep breath and confidence filled her brain. She would strive for excellence and stop only when the answer was sitting in front of her, packaged and tied up with a neat bow.

It was soon after she was back at her desk that someone knocked on the door to the office. She kept it locked. She knew who it was. Danny, the delivery man. She went over and unlatched the lock. The door opened and she quickly moved from its direction to avoid clashing with it.

"Oh hello," Danny said. His eyes shifted down towards the two packages he held in his hand. He smiled at her and asked, "Can you sign?"

She signed for the package and then casually asked him to come into the office. He started to make excuses about his busy day but she curtly said, "You were here on Monday. Have you heard? Mitch Greenway died that day." She was speaking loudly. Maybe it was to justify her words.

"Yes?" he asked, appearing confused.

"Greenway was in this office. He's a patient of the doctor here. Now listen," her voice descended to a whisper, "I'm not accusing you of anything, but I'd like to know a little information. What exactly do you deliver to Dr. Weihen?"

He shifted his eyes again. He knew how to play this out. Weihen was in his therapy room, so she pushed them further into the waiting room.

"Listen, Ms.—"

"Tulit," she corrected. She admired his dedication.

"Right. I don't know what you're talking about. I deliver my packages. That's what I'm assigned to do."

"Who supplies them?"

"The delivery company, IPS, of course."

"Does Weihen have contact with them? Do you have access to the inside of the package?"

"Shit, I don't know. I can't just open packages, I can tell you that. I'm the messenger, not the supplier. Are we done? I'm late on my run," he said. He was loud, and Dr. Weihen naturally heard. He came out and asked what was going on. Clara didn't expect it, but there was nothing to hide. The man offered no incriminating evidence. Weihen was in the clear with him.

"Nothing," she said to Victor. "Danny was just delivering some packages."

He nodded, said goodbye, and walked out of the waiting room. She gained nothing from their conversation, but perhaps that was good. She sensed he had nothing to do with the transfer of sample medicine to Weihen. Though she found it strange that samples came by a normal delivery service. Cifonide was probably not available to whatever medical company Weihen ordered from, anyway. It was only available from a chemical manufacturer. Leiman Turner was her man.

"I think there was only one package ordered today," Victor said. His eyes were fixed on some trivial thing in the room. He was probably searching his memory for the order.

"Perhaps they separate the order into two shipments. They sometimes do that, remember?" Clara held the packages tightly.

"Oh, it doesn't matter, anyway. It's not like there's any more patients to treat! It's all over, Clara. I'm just waiting to see if they arrest someone else. My only hope is that the real killer is found and my former patients can trust me again." His eyes teared every so slightly. Her stomach growled and she gave a slight burp. She was hungry. She needed to eat if she was going to confront Miles later that day.

Victor looked into her eyes and then rushed back into his office. He had entirely forgotten about the packages. She put them on the desk and opened them.

***

After Clara grabbed a sandwich from the deli across the street (one of those chain delis that was anything but "fresh"), she sat at her desk to eat. She didn't know what Victor was doing in his office, nor did she care. She was starving, though, so the subpar sandwich tasted fantastic. She ate it in those large bites for which the prime objective was not to taste the food, but to feel the biggest lump go down the esophagus and drop into the stomach. Every one or two bites was washed down with Coke. She was almost finished when Pearson and Suds came knocking on the office door.

"Why is the door locked?" Pearson asked.

"For good measure. There are killer's running about," Clara said wiping her mouth, as if it was a normal and expected thing to say.

"But isn't Weihen seeing patients?"

"They all cancelled—thanks to you. After seeing his name mentioned in the paper, and his possible connection with Greenway's untimely death, no one wants to see him anymore. Who wants to see a psycho psychiatrist?"

"Listen, uh—"

Her eyes rolled for yet another time that week. "Clara," she said. She thought about adding in *jerk*. Was he forgetting her name on purpose?

"Right. It wasn't our fault. We need to see Dr. Weihen once more. Just a few more things to clarify."

It was time to get information. "Before you arrest him?"

"I didn't say that." His eyes drifted to his notepad.

She pointed them to the office and they took the cue to go in. She took her usual stance: ear against the door.

Weihen said, "Oh hello, officers. What else can I do for you?"

Suds chimed, "Nothing special. We just need a list of the inventory that comes and goes from this office."

"Clara can get that for you, gentlemen."

She rushed back to her seat, quickly grabbing for the last bite of sandwich. She wouldn't risk being caught again. They came out as she was sitting down, out of breath, sandwich stuffed into her mouth. Air was going in and out of her nose rapidly, but she still felt like there wasn't enough.

She started to gather the inventory records for them and vaguely thought about where she put the boxes from earlier that morning. They were in the dumpster out back. When she retrieved the papers, she made photocopies and handed them over. She decided to seize her opportunity and mention something else.

"Listen, guys, I want to be honest. I don't think Victor is your man." In truth, she really didn't know what to believe anymore.

"Thank you, Clara, but don't jump to conclusions. We're not set on anyone yet."

She said, "I mean to tell you that I don't care what you're set on, I *know* he's not the one." It was funny that just an hour before she was convinced he was. Maybe she was just trying to piss Pearson and Suds off. "I am undergoing my own investigation to find the murderer."

Suds laughed, Pearson stared. "Alright, Claire." Wrong, again. "Don't get into trouble, and if you find any information or evidence, you need to report it to us, you hear? Otherwise your unlawfully tampering with an ongoing investigation."

They started to leave. "Just one more question. Where did you find the will?"

Suds let out a sigh and turned around. "Where did we find the will, boss?"

"At the kid's house." He directed his speech towards her. "At Miles Greenway's house. Why?"

"I don't know. I felt it was somehow important. Don't worry, it will fit together soon."

"Claire, I suppose you would want to know the autopsy was finished yesterday. It'll be in the news, so we might as well tell you."

She had forgotten about the autopsy. "Yes?"

"Poison, as expected. Found primarily in the mouth. Some chemical thing called cifonide. Very potent. Know anything about it?"

"Nothing at all," she lied.

Chapter Ten

After Clara left the office, she wanted to go back home and decompress before setting out on her next journey to interview Miles. To be honest, she wondered if she should be getting any information from these people. Was it safe? One of them had to be a killer. If the person already killed once, doing it again wouldn't be too hard. It would be important to get rid of the person who has too much information, especially if they were crying out that they wanted to solve the case.

The idea of her own death started to take over her mind again. *No one would remember her.* It repeated, like it was a mantra. Everyone would remember Mitch Greenway. There were already tributes and memorials popping up all over Houston. It had only been two days for God's sake! The funeral hadn't even happened yet. Greenway's second death would never come. He'd outlive Clara for sure. The great oil pioneer, the philanthropist. What would she be remembered for? The secretary to his psychiatrist. His possibly murderous psychiatrist. It wasn't fair. She would only be remembered if she made things right. Yes, it was her one chance. She could see it. The headlines would read, "CLARA TULIT:

THE WORLD'S FINEST DETECTIVE." Only in her dreams.

She got home and collapsed in the living room. Her mother was probably upstairs, Tracy wasn't awake yet. The girl wasn't entirely a morning person. Clara thought about bringing her along for Miles' interview, but she acted strange enough at the last one. It was unfortunate, the way she thinks. As if she knows exactly how an investigation is to be done because she reads books and watches television.

Perhaps Clara needed to engage her even more, though. She might be excited for the latest development: the poison was indeed cifonide. Turner wasn't lying—he was definitely the supplier. The police haven't figured that out yet, of course. But Clara knew. It was only a matter of time before he was a prime suspect. It seemed to her that the culprit had to be Turner or Mrs. Whittle if everything were to go her way. The delivery man seemed to have nothing going against him, so that avenue was gone. Of course, mom would have a lot on her if word got out and Victor would probably be arrested soon. She needed to focus on Turner and Whittle. It would be perfect. She had nothing to do with them and wouldn't care if either were sent away. If one of them *actually* did it, that would be double bonus points. There was just one more person to see before she could make a targeted approach at one of them. The case rested on if he was being blackmailed or not.

She dialed Miles' cell phone because she knew they weren't quite on a show-up-without-calling basis. Tracy might have been—she suddenly seemed to be pretty good friends with him. Beyond awkward dinners. Clara was not on the same level as her.

"Hey, Miles?"

"Who's this?" His voice was calm. No traces of grief. She supposed he never entered her phone number into his or he would have had caller ID.

"Oh, it's Clara… Tulit," It was strange saying her last name. They were family friends; they were friends! He should know her by her first name. Hell, he should have known her by her voice… or the caller ID, for that matter!

"Hello Clara. It was good to see you the other day—was that yesterday?"

"Yes," she said.

"I hope you're not calling about my father. Your family—especially your mom—has been so kind through this. Don't give any more apologies. I swear, I can't even bear to hear them from people anymore! Dying is natural. It happens to everyone. We must move on." He said his words apathetically.

"Oh, no. I *am* sorry, Miles. But I didn't call to say that." She fidgeted with the pillow on the couch. "I wanted to see if I could come over and ask you a few questions actually." Another brain spasm was coming on again.

"A few questions?"

Silence. She was just staring at the pillow. Break out of the trance. Come on. Her eyes shifted and she regained composure. "Yeah, just a few. Tracy and I had this little idea that we could figure out the entire murder case. One can't always trust the police to truly figure out these sorts of things, you know? They think that it might be Dr. Wei-hen. I told them they were crazy. Well, not literally…"

"You're acting as a detective in my father's murder?"

She didn't know how he would react. Would he care? "Yes. So I was wondering if I could ask just a few questions."

"I suppose," he said. "But remember, we must move on from this! We don't need to dwell in the past." She was put off by his lack of curiosity or even compassion. "Will Tracy be coming?" The pitch of his voice raised.

"Um, well…" She had to make a decision. "No, she hasn't woken up yet." It would be too distracting for Miles if she was there. They were too friendly.

He said, "Oh, okay. Are you going to take notes or something? You said you are both acting as detectives."

Notes. Why did he care? She said, "Right. Yeah, I'll take notes. I'm good at asking questions. Tracy is good at figuring out what the answers mean… Not that you'll be cryptic or anything. When can I come?"

"Stop by my house anytime this afternoon. The mansion is still a crime scene. Too much happening there."

It was funny that he referred to his parents' house as a mansion. His own house was quadruple the size of the one Clara lived in with her mom and sister.

"Okay," Clara said. When she hung up, she went to Tracy's room. Her sister was probably still asleep, but Clara knocked this time. It was already after twelve thirty, she needed to get up anyway. After hearing nothing, Clara opened the door to find her passed out in the bed. What a shock.

When she practically yelled Tracy's name, her sister comfortably rolled over with a smile on her face. Her eyes opened, and every bit of joyful emotion drained as she saw Clara standing in her room.

"Oh, hi." She had the glare of disappointment. Must have been having a good dream.

"It's after noon, Tracy," Clara said. She opened the blinds and rays of sunshine peered in. They looked dusty, illuminating the particles floating in the sour air. Perhaps the window needed to be opened, too.

Tracy was in her bathroom, door shut, when Clara announced she had interesting news on the case.

"And what is that?" Her mouth was full—she was brushing her teeth.

"The police figured out the poison. Cifonide." Clara waited for her to absorb the information.

"Cifonide? Where did I hear that again?" She was still brushing.

"Remember Turner admitted to taking it from Ashburn chemicals and giving it to Weihen?"

The sink stopped and the door opened. She had a wash cloth up to her mouth. "Oh my God! Mitch was officially killed by the stuff?"

"That's right. Leiman isn't looking too good. Still think he didn't do it?" Clara laughed.

Tracy scrunched her face. She was trying to make sense of it and said, "I *know* he didn't do it. You could tell. His mannerisms and, of course, his inability to cheat."

The stupid rules. Clara rubbed her face and said, "Are you kidding me, Tracy? You did nothing! That little apparent show that you gave hardly gives any indication of a man's murderous intentions. Leiman Turner had access to that toxin." She cooled down. "Maybe you're right. Maybe he didn't do it, but that means Weihen did and Turner is the supplier! He admitted it. Where else would you find cifonide?"

Tracy started to make her bed and finally opened the window. "Why are you asking me? I don't even know what cifonide is, let alone where you would find it. I think my afternoon shall consist of some important research. I want to know the effects of this toxin. What is it commercially used for? Medicine? Why does Ashburn manufacture it in the first place? This thing surely isn't going to schools. More importantly, who else would have access to it? Remember, Clara, the best murderers will always plan a diversion. It's done in every story imaginable. The trade-off could have genuinely been an innocent one."

Why would Weihen need cifonide if he wasn't killing Greenway? It wouldn't make sense. Clara didn't believe in coincidences. She replied, "Great. I have some, well, work to do this afternoon. Why don't you do that research and we'll meet up tonight."

Tracy looked at Clara, but didn't ask what her plans were for the day. She clearly wasn't invited, so she shrugged it off. "Dinner?" she asked.

"No, I think we should eat with mom tonight."

"Why?" she asked.

"She might be lonely, Tracy," Clara said. "Her lover just died. And besides, I want to know a few things about her planned trip."

Clara told her she would leave Tracy to her research and walked out, further neglecting to confide about the interview with Miles. It was about a half hour later that she finally decided to go over there. It was the usual: she picked up the keys and drove through the streets of beautiful trees. Eventually, she made her way to the land of the rich. Houses that either looked like museums or compounds. They always had a few cars parked out front. Porsches, mostly. There was a Ferrari in the entryway to the house that attempted to be modern, but just looked like a big bubble ready to pop.

Miles Greenway lived about five minutes away from his parents. Compared to their estate, his house was "small," but still quite a mansion. The architecture was *cool.* The entire outside structure was made of marble—it looked more like a giant statue than anything. A glorious fountain stood in the driveway, which was paved by tarnished brick. Clara saw his blue Mercedes (the brand was a favorite among the Greenways) parked off to the side. Her small Subaru didn't belong.

Everything Miles owned was funded by his parents. Of course, he went to the rich prep school that she and Tracy attended, but he went along to study at some prestigious university. A great school, but he was accepted for his wealth and he chose it because he didn't want to venture too far from his extraordinary life. And he was set for money, so what did it matter? Eventually he would take over the company.

Clara found herself applying more makeup while sitting in the driveway. The house looked too perfect— it needed to be filled with people who at least tried to be good-looking. She was always blessed with her natural looks, but she never really cared for appearance, so she always looked average. The glasses that covered her face were square and unappealing. Her hair was always tied up in a ponytail and she too often wore boring business attire. Yet, no wrinkles, a pretty face, and soft skin that was, for lack of better phrasing, easily tannable.

The doorbell scared the crap out of her when pressed. It sounded like a gong and echoed throughout the solid stone structure. The birds that had settled on her car thirty feet away went flying. She stood there knowing it would take a minute or two for Miles to answer the door. The house was *that* big.

"Coming." She heard his voice say through the little telecom. He opened the door forty seconds later.

"Hi," she said. She went in after his gesture. "How are you holding up?"

"Oh, Clara." He sounded relaxed, calm. Maybe they were better friends than she thought. Not just acquaintances? "It's hard." He said it like a reflex.

The inside of the house remained pristine. Often, one would imagine a person who lost his father to be a little messy. Not a hair was out of line on his thick head, or a wrinkle on his Ralph Lauren custom-fitted button down shirt.

He led Clara into the living room, where they sat for the rest of the time.

"I know all too well what you're going through," she said. "When my dad died, I felt like the world was over. It wasn't fair, I thought." She didn't say it, but that's when she stopped practicing religion. No god would be that selfish. "Of course, he wasn't murdered." The words came quickly and she felt their awkward percussion. Everything echoed in the house.

He poured himself a glass of whatever alcohol was on the coffee table. "Want some?" She shook her head. It smelled like whiskey, but it was much too early in the day. "So," he said, getting comfortable. "What did you want to talk about?"

"Well, you know, I'm investigating this whole thing myself. Your father is a friend to our family, but I'll be honest, it's not because of that." Not a twitch from him. "You see, I don't know what you know or if you're keeping up, but the police think Dr. Weihen may be the guy. You may not know him well, but I do. And I have a strong feeling he didn't kill your father."

"Now how the hell do you know that, Clara?" His voice sounded collected and deadly, as if he had a point to make that would shatter her entire argument (which was already nonexistent). "I'm not so sure this Weihen man is innocent. Sure, father's been seeing him for a while, but what does it matter? These psychiatrists—they can go crazy, too."

He was just like her sister. He had been consumed in the murder mystery culture and was flouting his supposed knowledge. No wonder Tracy had more things in common with him than Clara did.

He said, "I don't know much about the man. I do know the weapon was poison. Cifonide, they tell me. I have no idea what that is, but I do know a man of medicine is capable of acquiring chemicals. It's natural. Who else did my father come in contact with that day?"

"I don't know," she said. "You tell me." She was

going to hard-ball him.

"What is that supposed to mean?"

"Nothing, I just wanted to see if you knew anything else. You said you made a phone call to him. When was that?" She placed the tip of her pencil to her pad. He was aware that she was arriving at something.

"It was after his appointment."

"Time?"

"I don't know, eleven? A few minutes after. I called him to see if he wanted to do anything after the appointment. Maybe go golfing," he said.

"Why would he? He once told me that he likes to be alone after his visits. He liked time to recover." Clara added, "And the country club is closed on Mondays."

"Well, I didn't know about that." His eyes shifted. She needed to tackle the bull.

"Why was he carrying around his will and why was it at *your* house, Miles?"

His eyes widened and he finished off the whiskey. "Didn't think you would know that, Clara." He smiled, his eyes piercing. Yet he was calm. "Surprised you don't know what was in the will. That is what's more important. Apparently, he was giving a sum to Weihen."

"But you didn't know that on Monday morning," Clara offered.

He stared. "Okay, you're right. I didn't know that." His voice was trailing. She needed to guide him through his confession.

"So," she said, long and assuming. "You didn't call him after his appointment, though, did you? No, you called him before. What did you find out? That he was getting a copy of his newly revised will early that day. Very early. Uncomfortably *early*."

He impulsively gulped and winced at the burn of the alcohol still in his throat.

"So you got worried, I surmise. Is this true?"

"Yes, Clara. Listen, my father and I haven't been on the best of terms lately."

"He started to doubt your ability to run the family company?" Clara asked. She was simply repeating what she overheard that night in the bar. Her eyebrows flinched up. Was she pushing him too hard? It was all just a confirmation of everything she had thought. Nothing was truly new.

"Yes. I didn't finish too well at college two years ago. Dad had to do some maneuvering…" His finger and thumb massaged each other in a dramatic gesture of money. "Just for me to graduate."

"I'm so sorry, Miles." She honestly wasn't. She had a strong distaste for people who slacked in school and paid their way out of it. Especially really privileged people going to really expensive schools. She was privileged and she eventually slacked, but she dropped out. The fair way.

"I thought that," his eyes started to tear, "that maybe he was changing my inheritance of the company. Maybe even my inheritance of some money. Cut it down, just a bit. He said that after his appointment, he was going to stop by and talk to me about something. It would only take five minutes. I thought he was going to explain it all to me. I was worried."

"He went to your house?" Clara was surprised.

"No, he never did. I *did* call him after his appointment. I wanted to know where he was. He said he was tired and we would talk another time. So I got in my car and drove to the mansion. I found him dead there." His eyes looked out the windows.

"And you—"

"I took the will before telling my mother to call the police. It was in his pocket. I learned some interesting things after reading it later that day. He was always clear to me about my inheritance. I was—I was just a little paranoid. Nothing changed. Weihen got something, though."

"How much?"

He swallowed. He was uncomfortable, nervous. She wanted to see if he would tell the truth.

"Five million, Clara. Five million. If the police think he killed my father, I will go after that son of a bitch." He poured himself another glass.

Chapter Eleven

The home telephone rang. It was so early, Clara hadn't gotten out of bed yet. She ignored the phone and let it go to voicemail. She rubbed her eyes and checked the time: seven in the morning. She slept through the night again peacefully, which was nice. But thoughts of the case flooded her mind immediately; they would not go away when she was awake. There were no more witnesses to interview, save for Victor. Was she going to interview Victor? She saw him quite enough, didn't she? It felt weird, but he *was* the primary suspect. All of the cards were against him in every aspect. And she wasn't satisfied with him being the killer quite yet. She was trying to prove he wasn't, for God's sake. But she was starting to realize how the entire case would play out— Victor was fighting an uphill battle. She wouldn't give up on her job. Not yet.

But she wanted to *know*. If anything, she wanted to be convinced it was him so she could have a sense of closure. There was no end at that point, and she had to keep going. The five million was a bit striking. After everything, she really didn't expect it. It was the cherry on top; Victor was doomed.

So what else could she do? She had greatly feared her search would come to a halt and it had. She walked into the bathroom and splashed the yellowish water on her face. Visitors from out of town looked at their water in disgust; Clara tried to explain the color was just from the minerals. Of course, she didn't really *know*, but it consoled them nonetheless. The phone rang again. It stopped after the second chime, so someone had to have picked it up.

She wouldn't go into work for the day. If she was going to interview Weihen, it would be tomorrow. The final interview. It would settle everything and after an analysis of facts, in close conjecture with Tracy, who was now her colleague, the case would be solved. If it wasn't Victor (maybe even if it was), Clara would boldly walk into the police station and present the indisputable evidence in a glorious fashion. She would sweep them from under their toes and they would stand and applaud. Suds would have tears in his eyes, Pearson would shake her hand. But today—she didn't know what to do today. Perhaps an exchange of opinions and suspicions with Tracy. She could lend one of those ridiculous thriller novels and Clara would finally understand what goes on in her head. Maybe it was good there wasn't much to do. Clara felt relaxed. But then her mom walked into the room.

"Honey," she said. "So glad you're awake." Her hand was covering the bottom half of the phone and was quivering. "There's a phone call for you." And then in an almost unreadable whisper, "It's the police."

Clara was genuinely surprised. She didn't know what they could be calling about and foolishly answered in a perky manner. She grabbed the phone, shooed mom out, and said, "Hello? This is Clara."

There was a throat clear. The voice said, "Ms. Tulit, this is detective Pearson. There's been a new, um, *development*. We're going to need you to come down to the station."

Her eyes grew excited. "A development? What kind of—" She stopped as a new question formed in her head. "Wait, why do *I* need to be at the station?"

She could hear him sip his morning coffee. A slurp that lasted an eternity. "Well, Ms. Tulit, I'll actually need you and your sister to come down."

"Tracy? What happened?"

"Ms. Tulit, there's been another murder." Clara's face grew pale. He said, "She was in the presence of Greenway the day he died. A patient of Dr. Weihen's. Name is Angela Whittle."

She could feel something pumping through her veins—was it adrenaline? The murderer had struck again. She was just a lonely, old lady. Clara took a long time to digest it, but she before the detective hung up the phone.

"But—but how?"

"Well, Ms. Tulit, that's what we're trying to figure out. You see, you and your sister's fingerprints were found in her apartment. They're fresh, maybe only a few days only."

Clara's eyes were big as she was taking in the information. Almost panting, she said, "No, no. My sister—we were looking for Greenway's killer. We were interviewing Mrs. Whittle."

"I figured as much," he said. "Listen, Clara, you

should leave these cases to the professionals like me. Like I said, you're tampering with an investigation."

But the police were doing nothing! He didn't even know the connection Whittle had to the case. She very much could have been the killer herself. Then the thought lingered in Clara's head. If she revealed that Whittle was blackmailing Greenway to the police, she would certainly have to admit what it was all about. They would learn about mom. She had to keep it to herself, and warn Tracy to do the same.

"I suppose so," she said. A million thoughts were running through her head.

"Anyway, we want you down to the station. Not because you're suspects, but because we know that you recently spoke to Whittle about all this. For obvious reasons, we are assuming whoever killed Greenway killed Whittle. She must have had a little too much information on her hands. We need to hear exactly what she told you at your meeting."

"Okay." She was eager to get off the phone and speak with Tracy. "We'll be there in a half hour."

"Ask for Pearson at the desk." The dial tone was quick to chime. It was going to be a trade off. Of course they were suspects—but they weren't going to be if they offered up information. She had no time to lose, so she went straight to Tracy.

Naturally, her sister was in bed sleeping. Clara barged in and nudged her until she woke. "Tracy," Clara said. "You need to get up. We need to be at the police station in a half an hour."

"What?" She sprung up. Clara had suspicions that

she was faking her deep sleep so she would go away.

"That's right. Mrs. Whittle is dead. We were the last ones to speak with her—they need our input."

"Oh my!" She hopped out of the bed, clearly excited. "I need to—I need to gather my thoughts. What *did* Whittle say?" She was rushing to her notepad. All of the two pages that were actually used in her notepad.

Clara gave Tracy a stern look. "She said a lot, Tracy! She said a lot. She knows about mom's affair, remember? She was blackmailing Greenway, remember? For the longest time, I though *she* was the killer!"

"You're right," she said. "I even noted it in my pad! There were clear indications. Now she's dead?"

Clara nodded, eyes focused. "She's dead. And that's a whole other conversation because now there are only three suspects. Well, four if you include Danny, the delivery guy. But I don't think he's involved."

Tracy wasn't listening carefully. It looked like thoughts were running behind her eyes a million miles an hour. She said, "What a development!"

"Listen Tracy," Clara said. She tried to speak over her sister's excitement; Tracy really loved these detective games. "Whittle knew about mom's affair. The police *cannot*. You understand? We keep it to ourselves. We say that Whittle was a dead end. Just a little old lady who saw Dr. Weihen for her OCD. We'll say she mentioned something about blackmail, but no specifics. We didn't believe her at the time. Comprendo?"

Tracy nodded.

The driveway. The trees. A turn onto Dunlavy and then Richmond, and onto the police station.

The Houston Police Department was situated downtown, about a fifteen minute drive. Clara and Tracy were both silent as they were contemplating what they would say when the time came. She didn't even know if they would interview them separately as if they *were* suspects. She tended not to believe the police. She would have liked to think they wouldn't waste their time like that—or hers. Just because they were not doing their job didn't mean Clara and Tracy couldn't be back out there finding the next clue. Some small part of her hoped that Pearson and Suds had just given up and were calling them down to acquire the information the sisters had gathered.

Of course, it was a tricky situation. Clara was going through what information she *could* offer them. Nothing could be connected to mom. She imagined Tracy was doing the same thing. The big reveal would be Leiman Turner and his job at the chemical company. The second would be that Whittle mentioned she had information and was blackmailing Greenway, but never told them what that information was. *Even after intense provoking, she wouldn't give in*, she would say.

Finally, as much as Tracy would probably hate to hear it, Clara was going to tell them the aggression that Miles had exhibited all through the case. From their first meeting on Tuesday to their remote interview the day after, he had been unemotional and seemingly unaffected. That had to indicate something. Besides, he said he would go after Weihen—wasn't that a threat? Lucky she was taping their conversation like she did with Turner. It was so easy to get little recorders nowadays—

she bought it down at the Spy Emporium, where she also got the camera for Weihen's office.

Halfway through the drive, she became worried when Tracy said, "Mom's been getting more hysterical every day." Clara understand her compassion but this was no time to be thinking about mom. She needed to be thinking about evidence.

"Huh, I hadn't noticed," Clara said mindlessly. Of course, she had. Their mother was practically sobbing at the dinner table the night before. She couldn't stop scouring the internet for every article, tribute, and video about the great Mitch Greenway. She idolized him to the extent that it was borderline creepy; Clara felt bad for her.

Clara for once felt guilty about lying when she told mom that all of the evidence was gone. She organized everything her mom had given her and thinks she burned. The tickets for the flight, and everything else that came along with them. Fake IDs, passports, and the credits card under two aliases. Abigail and Carl Richmond. In reality, Clara put the materials in a shoebox in her room. She didn't quite know what to do with them at that moment, but she somehow felt the need to keep them. At least she knew no one was going through the shoes in her closet.

When they pulled into the station, Clara felt well prepared. She couldn't say the same about Tracy, though. Tracy looked like a bundle of nerves, shaking and twitching ever so slightly. As they walked in, Clara maintained a firm, entitled walk. Eyes up, she never made contact with any officers lingering about; she went straight to the desk where a red-haired lady was staring at a computer. She continued to stare.

Staring. Nothing else. Clara looked at Tracy, whose eyes were all over the place. She stepped on her foot in a warning kind of way: *you have to stop looking nervous*. How could she be nervous? It's not like she is connected to any crime—she, like Clara, was trying to *solve* the crime. One that the police weren't solving very well. But that's how it was, she supposed. The innocent acted the most guilty; the guilty acted the most innocent. Police knew this too, she wasn't just making it up. She was absolutely positive they would be fine.

"Eh-hem," Clara coughed. The lady finally looked up.

"How can I help you?" she said, followed by several slaps of gum chewing. The kind that opens the mouth as big as it can and then quickly jerks it closed.

"We were called to see Detective Pearson and, um, his partner."

"Have a seat." Two minutes later, she dialed the phone and called him out.

"Clara, good to see you," Pearson said, walking into the reception area. He remembered her name. "You must be her sister, Tracy."

"Hello," Tracy said, shaking hands.

"Follow me."

They were lead through a hallway into a plain room the size of an average business office. It had a table in the center, a few chairs, and really nothing else. Not even a window.

"Coffee?" Pearson asked. After they shook their heads, he shot them a *suit yourself* look and left the room.

"You ready, Tracy?"

"Yeah," she said. "This really is no big deal. We just need to present the evidence we have."

"Except—"

"Except anything about mom."

Pearson walked in with one of those small, cheap styrofoam cups that often added a weird plastic taste to whatever liquid was inside. Whenever she drank out of one, she would bite the edge and it would be ruined quickly. She never liked those stupid cups. Suds came in after Pearson and they both sat down. The next few words were exactly what she wanted to hear.

"Listen, girls, we thank you for trying to give the case a go." Detective Pearson sat down, practically collapsing into the chair. His eyes were tired. "All we want is to hear what you know. We never got the chance to talk to this Whittle lady. Tell us what she said and everything else you've acquired. We'll handle it from there, and we request that you stop your mock investigation. Easy?"

Tracy nodded. Clara was unsatisfied. Of course she would continue to investigate; she was the one who was going to *solve* the case, she thought. Just wait; they would see. It would be indisputable when she presented the truth to them. She wanted to get an award.

"And what if we don't?" said Tracy. Clara stole a sharp look at her.

"You don't want to play that game, ma'am," said Suds. He was standing, leaning against the wall behind Pearson, crappy styrofoam cup in hand.

"Well." Her eyes were excited, voice playful. "It's not like we're *arrested* or anything. We can walk out whenever we want."

Clara understood what she was getting at, but they didn't discuss it beforehand.

"Besides, how could you trust two girls' information? If you used our data, it would certainly make you look incompetent," she continued.

"Ma'am, I—"

"Don't ma'am me, officer Pearson. I see what you're doing here. You act like you *want* our information, as if we're nothing more than 'kids' just playing around. But you know that's not true. You're worried we're not just having fun with this. Well, we're not and we won't stop until we know the truth! Just because you can't seek any *real* answers doesn't mean that we can't. I know exactly what you're doing! Both of you are worried that we're doing more work than you! We have had three suspect interviews so far."

"Four," Clara chimed. Perhaps she would go along with it.

"Four?"

She nodded. She had told her earlier.

She said, "Four suspect interviews! How many have you done?"

They sat in silence.

"I thought so." She pursed her lips into a grin. "You know why? Because no one wants to bother talking to the police, officer Pearson. You're too intimidating." She laughed. "No, they are much more willing to talk to ordinary people who seem somewhat invested in a case. Anyway, you think we'll solve the case before you, possibly mention to another detective at the office, and you'll be mocked, laughed at! Isn't that right?"

She was really on a roll. Clara honestly did not know how to react.

Pearson sipped his coffee. "No, ma'am. We just want to solve the case. You knew Mrs. Whittle. Will you tell us anything about her? If not, leave and we'll carry on." The excitement of Tracy's speech had completely died out.

The two girls shifted in their seats and began telling them all they wanted to tell them.

"Fine. Whittle had been blackmailing Greenway for an unknown reason. She wouldn't tell us," Tracy said.

"That's right," Clara said, "Clearly she knew something she shouldn't have known."

Pearson nodded every so often as they spoke. Suds was quickly writing in his pad. The discussion continued. Mrs. Whittle, Leiman Turner, and even the delivery man were mentioned. They didn't say anything about Turner's confession; they just mentioned his noteworthy job and that Ashburn Chemicals manufactured cifonide. Clara decided to not mention Miles.

"Delivery man?" Suds asked. "You didn't mention any delivery man in your initial report, Ms. Tulit."

"I—I must have forgotten. It was a stressful time," she said.

"What is his name?"

"Danny. I don't know his last." She already regretted mentioning the delivery man. They were just going to annoy an innocent man. "Really, he has nothing to do with the case. I spoke to him. He knows nothing. I'm pretty good at getting someone to crack."

Pearson inquired, "Where does this Danny work? Who does he deliver from?"

"A delivery service. IPS, I believe. Ask Weihen about it."

"We will," Suds said, eyes on his pad.

"Anything else, Ms. Tulit?" Pearson's gaze shifted between Tracy and her. "Ms. Tulit?"

They both agreed there was nothing else to say. They had covered everything they wanted to. It was obvious Tracy was a little disappointed by the whole experience. She wanted to be that tough gal that pushed envelopes to seek justice. Pearson flat out rejected her. She read too many of those books.

Pearson stood and picked up the now-empty coffee cup. He looked at his partner and said, "Well, thank you ladies. Despite what you may think, we really are trying to get to the bottom of this case. Suds is sort of new to the job, as I told Clara. He's been around about a year. Eager to impress, ain't that right?"

"Yes, sir," Suds said.

Pearson continued, "This Turner looks like a good avenue to explore. Now that Whittle's out of the picture. And ladies, don't think we're not doing our own bits of discovery. There's a certain item we found on the body that we're further exploring."

The lipstick, Clara thought. Why would it be suspicious? It could easily have been for Linda.

Pearson said, "And Weihen isn't the only one on our radar. He tipped us off to a little secret. There was another person in the office that day."

Clara felt a rush. Excitement, maybe? She said, "Another person? Impossible. I was there. I saw everyone. No one could have went through that front door without being inspected by my eyes."

"Yes, well Ms. Tulit, you don't know everything. Or you've seemed to have missed this," he said with a grin.

"Who was it?"

He said, "The damn fellow wouldn't give us the name. He's stupid like that. If he would cough it up, his image may be cleared."

"Did he say *anything* about this other person?" asked Tracy.

Pearson cleared his throat and desperately looked into his cup for another drop of coffee. There wasn't one. He said, "Well, apparently this guy is a psychopath. Weihen knew about this in secret and didn't tell anyone else. He wouldn't give any more information. We concluded that he must have been treating this man 'behind the curtain,' so to speak. Not surprised you don't know about him, Ms. Tulit."

Clara was in absolute shock. There was no secret patient. Or was there? How could she not know? It had to be made up. A fabrication by Victor to save him from being arrested and possibly convicted. That would explain the ambiguity; no name, no specifics. All she knew was that she needed to speak with Victor soon.

Chapter Twelve

*C*lara and Tracy made their way out of the station and Tracy seemed even more animated than before. It was beyond Clara how she could ever look at a situation like this with exhilaration.

Clara said, "You look cheerful, don't you? After you were shut down with the whole *you need us* spiel."

She laughed as she descended the five steps down into the parking lot. "Hey, I thought I'd give it a shot, you know?" Her laugh stopped, but her smile widened. "And did you hear? A secret psychopath? How perfect! All we need to do is figure out who this man is. We are coming to the climax of this investigation, Clara. You should be excited, too."

Excited, she was not. Surprised, indeed. She couldn't help but think why she held back the information about Turner—somewhere in her, she was still protecting Weihen. It was discomforting to her. The police now knew that Turner worked at the chemical company, Ashburn. And they knew that Ashburn produced cifonide. It would be a perfect lead for them. They just didn't know he gave it to Weihen. Perhaps they already think he poisoned Greenway himself with it. Maybe Weihen would walk.

Nevertheless, it was a lead for them to explore, most likely with a dead end. He gave it to Weihen and the police didn't know it. It would keep Pearson occupied and off her back.

They stopped for lunch at one of the newer hipster places that promised only the freshest and healthiest ingredients. The ingredients may have been healthy, but the portions were certainly not. She watched Tracy bring the tray of sandwiches to the table. She grabbed the drinks—two diet cokes.

Tracy flipped her hair back and manhandled her sandwich all the way to her mouth. A colossal bite ensued. Chewing, she said, "So what's the next plan of action?"

"I think I seriously need to pay a visit to Dr. Wei-hen—but that can wait until tomorrow. There needs to be an incredible amount of planning that goes into that. Every question needs to be answered. Especially ones about the furtive psychopath."

She was already done with half of the sandwich. "Just you? No help from me?"

"Oh—" Clara couldn't risk taking her to see Victor. She was defending the man, but it would be risky. "Well, you will be help. You'll assist in planning. As for the actual interview, I should go alone. Victor knows me and surprisingly opens up really well to me. If you're in the room, he might be less generous, if you know what I mean."

"Okay." Tracy rolled her eyes. Clara was being the protective big sister. She was like that all the time. But that was her role, and she would stick with it.

"I can't believe there might be another person involved. I planned the whole damn thing out! We would interview all the 'witnesses,' and determine from there. I did not account for someone else to be in the running of suspects. I don't even *know* this person. And they're a psychopath? Well, now it looks like I'm—we're—not going to be the heroes, are we? The police knew about this man before we did!" Clara took a bite of her sandwich. She was ranting, but it felt so good to get her worries off her chest. She washed it down with the beautifully sweet, cold beverage. "We need to know everything in this case, you know? If we don't, then we're at a disadvantage. We'll never find out who killed Mr. Greenway. I just hope there are no more secrets lurking in the dark. Surely, we'll miss them. And then where will be?" Another bite politely landed in her mouth. She ate with manners, unlike her sister.

Tracy had been engrossed in her sandwich until Clara mentioned new secrets. That seemed to have perked her attention. Her smile became a look of deep thinking. Her demeanor was serious.

"You're right. *We* need to know everything," she said. She wasn't chewing anymore.

"That's right." Clara finished her sandwich.

They sat there for a few more minutes, mindlessly discussing trivial things. Tracy had mentioned that after all this was over, she would write a novel based on it. Clara could see she wasn't committed to conversation, though. She was fiddling her hands quite rapidly. Something was on her mind. Maybe Clara was shutting her out too much with the whole Weihen thing. She couldn't go, that was a given.

"A novel?" Clara said.

"Yeah." Clara tried to meet her sister's eyes, but they were elusive. Confidently, Tracy said, "I can't be lying around the house anymore. I need to *do* something. This is my perfect chance. If we solve this case, it's a true crime novel! Could you imagine *me* a true crime writer?"

No.

"Yes," Clara said. "It perfectly suits you. I mean, you almost had a bachelor's in English before you left school. Put that knowledge to use."

"Exactly." Her mind was still gone.

They left the place and drove home to find their mother passed out on the couch. A lovely sight. She had started drinking a little bit more than usual after Mitch's death, but not to this extreme. The sisters looked at each other, laughing a little. They never saw mom drunk before. Two bottles of wine lay next to her. A third on the table, three quarters empty.

"Shall we fix this mess?" Clara said.

"You do it," Tracy said. "I have something I need to do. I'll be back." She raced upstairs. It was curious, Clara thought. What was going on with her?.

She walked over and picked up the empty wine bottles first, then took a swig out of the third. She deserved a little something, right? Then, she nudged her mom, whose eyes opened, slowly and heavily.

"Wh—what are you doing?"

"Waking you up, mom," Clara said.

"Why? It's the middle of the night."

"It's the middle of the afternoon." Clara gave a small laugh. Her mom laughed too, ending with an unflattering snort. Then they were both laughing. Mom was quickly up and energetic on the couch, giggling and asking about Clara's day—or *night*, she joked.

"It was fine," Clara said. "And yours?"

"Fine." She looked at the wine bottles with a small pain in her eyes. They both sat back on the couch, silent for a few minutes.

Clara could hear Tracy pacing upstairs. Her room was directly above the living room. It sounded like she was speaking to someone, but Clara could have been mistaken. No one was upstairs unless mom started the habit of letting strangers into the house.

The affair popped into her mind. She didn't understand her mom's thought process when deciding to see Mitch. Was she doing it for the money or did she genuinely love him? Clearly not for the money, if they were planning to run away together. Though, they arranged to return two weeks later. Perhaps it was just a fling—a vacation. It was only two weeks, anyway. And then they would get back to their normal lives of sneaking around. She didn't think her mom would just leave Tracy and her out of the blue. The tickets brought them to the south of France. Marseilles. Mom always wanted to go there. She would try to convince her dad, but he said there wasn't any money for it. How was there no money? They lived in a nice house in a rich neighborhood. They may not have been the Greenways, but they were pretty wealthy.

"Hey mom," Clara said in a serious tone.

"Yes, honey." She was starting to doze off again. She

had switched the television on, but muted it. She probably didn't want to hear the sounds.

"Do you think you'll be remembered after you die?"

Her mother looked at her with an emotionless face. "Why do you ask? Really, sweetie, don't try to push me into a post-midlife crisis."

Clara gave a fake laugh. "No, it's not that. It's just, if I died today—if the killer came for me—I think that my influence would die pretty quickly. Perhaps it would die as soon as you and Tracy and went. You know what I mean? There's so many other people that will be remembered for so much longer. United States presidents, Egyptian pharaohs, celebrities…" She trailed off, thinking. "Even the bad guys, unfortunately."

"It doesn't matter, Clara, you'll be dead," she said before letting go and falling asleep.

"I suppose you're right," Clara said anyway.

She then proceeded to drag her mother up to the bedroom. It was one of the most difficult tasks ever endured. Her mother was half-awake, half-asleep, but offered no help in terms of using her muscles. She remained limp as Clara pulled her arm around her shoulder. It took at least fifteen minutes for them to actually get in her room. By that time, Clara was sweating and panting. She wanted a shower.

As she was walking to her own room, Tracy jumped out of her door. Her face looked nervous, riddled with anxiety.

"What's the matter?" Clara asked.

Tracy glanced at her phone for a split second. She looked up and said, "Oh, nothing."

The doorbell rang. It scared the hell out of Clara, but Tracy seemed to expect it. She started running down the stairs to open the door. What could possibly be the next little scheme she had going? And then Miles Greenway's voice ringed through the air.

Clara rolled her eyes. She couldn't talk with *him* anymore. There was nothing else to say. He was emotionless about his father's death and severely wanted Dr. Weihen to be convicted. He offered no evidence. She just had that bad feeling that he was connected in some way.

"Clara!" Tracy yelled. "Come down! Miles Greenway is here." She desperately did not want to come down. If Tracy invited him over, why did she need to accompany them? Slowly descending the stairs, she thought about the shower that wouldn't happen for at least another hour.

He was dressed wonderfully, as usual. A black suit and his father's camelhair coat. How could he be wearing that? Of all the coats. He could just buy another one, and yet he's using the coat his father died in. Strange.

"Hi Miles."

He shot a nervous glance similar to the one Tracy wore on her face since lunch. "Hello, Clara," he said. He took off his coat and handed it to Tracy.

"Come in," Clara said. They walked into the living room, where she quickly noticed she hadn't actually disposed of the wine bottles. She hurriedly started to pick them up, but had only gotten the two empty ones before Miles rushed to pick up the third. He noticed it was a quarter full and took two large sips. It was soon empty.

"That was my mom's," Clara said.

"Sorry. It looked good."

"I'm sure she doesn't care." It's not like *anyone* would really care.

When she got back from throwing out the wine bottles, Tracy and Miles were sitting on the couch next to each other.

"Sit down," Tracy said. She did.

"We—um—we have something to tell you, Clara," Miles said, looking at Tracy.

Clara raised her eyebrows, expecting them to go on. They sat in silence for about a minute as they fumbled to decide who would tell her this "something." Her brain started running through scenarios, but by their tone, she had expected it was the worst. They were seeing each other, she thought. She exhaled dramatically to remind them that they still needed to spit out whatever it was they wanted to tell her.

Tracy took the lead. "Well, Clara, we've been trying to hide it, but perhaps it is too dangerous to keep secrets after all that has happened. It will just slow down our investigation. Miles, charming Miles, and I have been seeing each other as of late."

She knew it! But she was pissed. "Seeing each other? How could you not tell me? Wh— I can't believe. Tracy, this is not okay. You're now further connected to the Greenways." Miles crossed his legs. He looked uncomfortable. "Though I don't see how you can be a suspect in the eyes of law enforcement. You didn't have any kind of grudge against Mitch, so it should be fine." Her thoughts were flowing out loud. Tracy and Miles were trying to keep up.

Tracy flinched and said, "Well, there are just a few, minor things that might be—" She stalled as she couldn't come up with anything. Eventually, she said, "—worthy. Worthy to, um, note. Things that might be worthy to note." She sat awkwardly, letting Miles take the lead now.

All he could muster was, "That's right."

Clara frowned. What could be against them? If she didn't know about their relationship, certainly no one else did. She inquired, "And what might those *things* be?"

Miles said, "Well, for starters, the lipstick."

Her mind made assumptions again and she concluded that they were both idiots. But she was now a bit more worried for them. "Go on."

"The lipstick found in my father's coat pocket. That was meant for Tracy."

"How?"

He said, "I was wearing my dad's coat the day before when Tracy texted that she needed lipstick for that night. We were going out. She doesn't have a car and didn't want to tell you about our relationship yet. So she called me. I picked it up... but I left it in the coat." He sounded embarrassed.

"Your dad's coat? Don't you have like a million coats! Couldn't you have gotten *another* coat?" They looked at her as if she was overreacting. She certainly was not. The case was falling apart as she knew it. Sure, Tracy still didn't have anything concrete against her, but there were still secrets being held.

"What else?" Clara asked. They looked at each other for the twenty-seventh time. She rolled her eyes and crossed her arms. "Tell me the whole story. The Tracy-

Miles relationship from the beginning."

Tracy took the lead. "Well, I suppose it started a year ago." She was smiling as memories flooded her brain. "We were having one of the family dinners. You went to bed early because you had an interview the next day. You were still looking for jobs then."

"I remember," Clara said, aggravated.

"Yes, well." She continued, "Linda, Mitch, and mom were in the dining room, drinking wine and laughing. Miles and I wanted out of there. We agreed," she giggled. "We both agreed immediately that it was not fun to be around drunk parents."

"They weren't even that drunk," Miles added.

"But we scurried away. Not to the living room, but upstairs. To my bedroom. Things just kind of felt right up there. All of a sudden we weren't talking about our futures anymore. We were writing our future." Tears rushed to her eyes. Clara felt like she wanted to puke.

"Very poetic, my dear," Miles mentioned.

Clara said, "So you've just been sneaking around this whole time? Why didn't you mention anything? Why didn't you tell *me*, Tracy?"

Tracy's emotion faded. "Well, that's where it gets a little complicated. We did tell. But only one person."

"My father," Miles interrupted.

"Yes," Tracy said painfully. "He was polite to me but it was clear he disapproved. He ordered us to tell no one else."

"Why would he disapprove?"

"I haven't the faintest clue," Miles stated. He was lying, Clara could tell.

"So what happened?"

"We said we would be married," Tracy said, grinning.

There was no time for analysis. There was no time for emotion. Clara once again needed more information. She couldn't condemn Tracy yet. Not until she got the rest of the facts.

Her eyebrows raised. "And he disapproved of that as well?"

Miles said, "Yes. That's right. We told him in the beginning of December, a month ago." His eyes were shifting. "But when he rejected, we maintained we would see it through. So—um—when I saw him fooling around with the will, I thought he was writing me out of the picture."

"Why is that?"

"Because we had set a date."

"A *date*?" Clara yelled. "You were going to get married without telling me, Tracy? Unbelievable. How could you? When is the goddamn date?" She was breathing through her nose.

Tracy started to talk again. "I'm sorry, Clara, but I couldn't tell you. We couldn't face anymore opposition. We would do it in secret and then let everyone know. That's what we decided. It would be for the best."

"Don't tell me you're already married." Her eyes were as wide as an owl's.

"No. The wedding is in a little less than two weeks. We arranged for the minister to come to Miles' house. Just the three of us. Unfortunately, Mitch found out and so Miles became worried with the will."

"And did he write you out of the will?"

"No."

Everything was flashing before her and she thought about giving up out of frustration. It was a helpless feeling—the same she had when hearing the news of Greenway's murder. Tracy's motive was easy: kill the bastard so they retrieve their inheritance upon marriage. They get the money. They didn't care about Mitch because he didn't care about their relationship. If they thought he was changing his will, they had an even stronger reason to poison him. Mom and Tracy now both had motives and she was the one who was supposed to keep it a secret? The case was becoming too big for her grasp. No one was innocent. She felt herself suffocating. Tracy and Miles were staring at her. It was the first time she truly believed that a family member of hers (whichever one) could be guilty. She didn't know what to think.

Chapter Thirteen

*C*lara pretended to hyperventilate and catch her breath, which allowed her to tell Tracy and Miles that she needed to lay down. In truth, she just wanted to get out of that living room.

"Do you want some water? I'll get it," said Tracy, sounding a bit surprised. She probably never saw Clara anxious. She rarely felt or showed any anxiety at all. But she thought she made a pretty convincing attack. She had the faintest worry that people might not actually hyperventilate during anxiety attacks, but she was almost sure they did.

"No, no. I'll—" Clara made a wave of her hand around her head to show she wasn't thinking straight. "I'll get some myself upstairs."

She walked to the archway that connected the living room to the entrance hall. About four feet from the stairs, she turned around, swallowed dramatically, and said desperately, "Please tell me that you mentioned everything. No more secrets?"

Both nodded.

"Good. I'll make sure you're both not screwed." And with that, Clara ascended the stairs. Nothing but silence seeped from the living room and she was aware that her opposition could easily have created a small rift in their relationship. Did she care? Certainly not.

Finally, she could have that shower. She twisted the slightly rusted knob to the hottest setting. She escaped her clothes quickly, but not before steam was rising above the glass shower frame and the mirror looked like a white canvas.

After some deep reflection, Clara decided two things; she would find the psychopath and ditch saving Weihen. She couldn't protect three people from this case. If the police wanted to convict him, it was fine by her. She would much rather be without occupation than family. Even if her family was clearly twisted and full of lies.

Her father would have never stood for this. He always managed risk. And by managing, he made sure there was no risk whatsoever. Everything he did, it was either to make money or break even. Never lose. Clara was thankful he gave those qualities to her. Tracy, on the other hand, was not as lucky. Clara wondered about her sense of responsibility. She supposed her sister could have never known Mitch would die, but she could have at least made someone in *her* family aware of it. Clara gave her mom a little more leeway—she had lost dad five years ago. Clara didn't believe in living in the past—it was time for her mother to move on. But an affair with a married man? That was below her. It was below him.

It was in the shower that Clara feared what could have easily been the truth. Yes, fear—an emotion she didn't feel often before the murder. Sure, the cops would find their victim and Clara would wrap enough evidence around one of the suspects to present her case. But she would never accuse her mom or Tracy. What if they did it? Did they deserve freedom?

Dad died from a heart attack. He was fifty-three years old, so it was quite unexpected. Almost surreal. The doctor said his diet was a bit unhealthy—he ate a lot of steak, even for a Texan. They never predicted there would be major complications so soon, though. Clara was the one who found him unconscious in the bathroom. He locked it, but after living in that house for twenty two years, she knew she could stick a pencil through the hole and it would unlock. He was in there unnervingly long and didn't answer when she knocked. She screamed, mom called the police, Tracy cried. In less than an hour, he was pronounced dead. Clara learned what despair felt like—being in a race car headed toward a cliff and having no control. He was such a kind, giving, and faithful man. Miles was now in the same position and Clara did not understand how he could be so calm.

The days turned into months after dad's death. And then years. After dropping out of school, Clara was looking for jobs. It seemed for a long time that she would never be lucky enough for a career. She was hopeful when she became a receptionist—now that was gone too. Tracy was even worse—she still never rebounded. Not a single job after her decline.

She could feel the disappointing coldness after turning off the hot water. Her hand reached for a towel. She dried her hair and signed her name on the foggy mirror. She did it every day.

Her priorities were set. She would push off the final interview with Weihen. He was already a good enough suspect. The first thing she would do would be to tell the police about Turner's confession. He gave Weihen the toxin. She wanted to save that tidbit for her grand presentation, but all of that was not important anymore. Turner was one of her few last hopes. He would be convicted or he would help with the case against Weihen. Either way, her family stayed out of the timeline.

Then there was the psychopath. The unknown, vague psychopath that was probably a fabrication by Weihen. Or was it? Clara was only the receptionist for eight months. Perhaps it was too dangerous for Victor to let her know. If he existed, she would find him. After notifying the police, she would drive to the office and snoop through the files. There would surely be something to dig up. If not, there was always the camera footage to fall back on. That would be a promising way of catching him.

She wasn't even close to dry when she returned to the bedroom. She could feel the water dripping off her skin onto the carpet. She slid on sweatpants, a shirt, and collapsed onto the bed. She needed to notify the police, but it was hard to fight the fatigue.

She rolled over and noticed something on the floor by the door. It looked like a folded piece of paper. She picked it up—a note from Tracy.

"Clara, I didn't want to bother you. Miles just left. He wanted to say that the funeral was tomorrow morning. It is just family, but he invited us as well. His mother gave him permission for the invitation. Don't make plans." Signed Tracy.

Everything was moving so fast, she hadn't even thought about the funeral. She threw the note on the desk next to the cup with the crappy pen. Her phone started ringing just then.

It took a few rings before she could actually find the damn thing in her bag. "Hello?" she said, flustered after sliding the answer button as fast as she could.

"Clara?" the voice said. When she recognized him, she crossed her eyebrows. Why would he be calling her?

"Dr. Weihen?"

"Yes. Listen, Clara. You said you've been trying to figure out the Greenway case on your own." He said it as if she were a child playing games.

"That's right. I was trying to save you."

"Well, what did you tell the police?" He yelled. Perhaps he was desperate.

"What do you mean?"

He took a breath. "Don't get stupid with me, Clara. I know you've been speaking to the police." He was menacing. "They're asking all sorts of questions that I don't even know the answers to. They say Turner had access to the poison—this *cifonide* stuff. Well I had no idea. How does that have to do with me?" Lies.

"Yes, I found that out when I interviewed the guy. I told the police—there was nothing about you." More lies.

He said, "I don't believe you, Clara. What did Turner say? I want to know."

"All he said was that *cifonide* was manufactured at the chemical company he works for."

She couldn't tell him everything else. Even the police didn't know yet that Turner confessed to giving the poison to Weihen. They would know soon enough, though. She heard a click.

"Dr. Weihen?"

He grunted.

"Oh, I thought you might have hung up."

He paused, then resumed his attack mode. She was happy she wasn't with him in person. And she was thankful she could keep her calm. He said, "What did you know about Mrs. Whittle? They were mentioning blackmail. I had to deny it all."

"Wh—why? Yes, I interviewed Whittle. She talked about how she overheard something between you and Greenway. Was that right? Yes, you and Greenway. Then she started blackmailing him about this secret, I suppose."

"Goddamn Whittle!" he exclaimed to himself.

"You do know she's dead."

"Yeah, yeah. I do, Clara." He seemed to not care at all.

She wanted to wrap up the conversation. "Is there anything else? Because I really have some things to do."

"Clara, I want you to stay out of all this. The police are mindless, but they'll do their job. I won't be held responsible for this murder. But if you keep finding information that makes me look bad, even though I didn't do anything—well, things might get worse." He was denying that he had anything to do with it. It was all a bit too much.

"Okay," she said and hung up the phone. He seemed hostile and worried. Not someone she want to deal with, especially since he's a murder suspect. To be honest, he sounded very guilty. Clara really didn't want to go to the office tomorrow to get the files and have to run into him. But it was her duty to finish this case and protect mom and Tracy.

* * *

The drive back to the police station was silent. Clara never thought she would be there twice in one day. She didn't usually listen to music in the car because she was not entirely a music person in general. People would ask about her favorite band or favorite artist. She didn't know and she couldn't care less; how was that for an answer?

The station looked exactly as it did earlier that day—intimidating. But Clara knew nothing behind those walls was actually threatening. From her small experience with Pearson and Suds, no one inside was doing anything remarkable either. So she walked in like a savior, ready to give them the key to the case and perhaps end it for good.

"I'm looking for Detective Pearson," Clara said confidently.

The woman behind the desk was staring at her computer. She needed to finish the paragraph or sentence or whatever she was working on before she could acknowledge Clara's existence with an answer. So Clara banged the little hutch of the desk and said, "Listen, I need to see Detective Pearson and it's urgent."

Her eyes rolled from the screen to Clara and she sighed a deep breath. "I'm looking to see if he's available." She returned her eyes to the computer, not even recognizing her from the morning.

"Well, perhaps you could tell me that so it doesn't

look like you're just ignoring me." She was stressed and having some desk clerk get on her nerves was the last thing she wanted.

"Not here."

"What? Where is he?"

"Working a case," she said.

Clara said, "Listen, I know exactly what case he's working. You tell me where he is. I have valuable information. Information that will probably end this case. And it's a *big* case," she looked at the desk lady. Hopefully she would get the gist that the famous Mitch Greenway case needed to be solved. If it didn't, the police department would be humiliated.

"I don't care what you know about the case. I can't tell you where Detective Pearson is, okay? Would you like to leave a statement? I can have someone take your statement."

"No," Clara said. "I want to talk to Detective Pearson directly." She needed to know where Pearson was. Talking to Turner? Weihen? She gulped. What if he had already gotten to Miles? Everything was breaking down. She needed to save this ship.

She knew she needed to distract the lady at the desk but she didn't know how. There was no way the woman would move from her throne of a seat in front of that old computer. But she did notice that behind the desk was a giant mirror with fogged letters in the middle of it that read, "HOUSTON POLICE DEPARTMENT."

"Do you know when he'll be back?" Clara asked innocently.

"No, ma'am."

"Could you just check to see if there's anything on that computer will tell you?"

She rolled her eyes once again and agreed. At the moment Clara saw the screen change on her computer through the mirror, she took a picture with her phone. The lady looked at her.

"Oh, I just wanted a picture of the police department sign. It's beautiful." It sounded so strange.

The lady sighed and said, "There's nothing on here, ma'am." Clara thanked her and left promptly.

Back in the car, she brought up the picture. It took a lot of zooming and enhancing—luckily, she had a very nice quality phone. Brand new, with a great camera. She made an opposite pinching motion on the screen—sort of like a slow flick. The picture became bigger and the resolution adjusted after a few seconds.

She was scrolling through—millimeter by millimeter—the computer section of the reflection in the mirror. All of the words were backwards, but it was easy to point out what she was looking for. Luckily, the woman was doing what she was asked and not playing sudoku or some other worthless game. The page was on Agent Pearson's profile. All of his information was pulled up. But she just wanted his cell phone.

There were two numbers listed under his picture above what she presumed was his home address (which was too blurry to make out). After careful inspection and instinct, she decided the second number was his mobile. She carefully deciphered the backwards numbers. As she drove out of the station, she dialed them on her phone. Clutching the device between her shoulder and ear, she heard the first ring. And then the second. And then a man's gruffly voice exclaiming something entirely inaudible.

"Hello?" Clara said.

His throat cleared. "Who is this? How did you get this number?" It was detective Pearson.

"Pearson, this is Clara." There was a long pause.

"Clara? The secretary girl?" What an asshole. Clara, the person who was probably about to give you the information to solve the case.

She swallowed her anger. "Yes, that's the one. Listen, I need to speak with you right away regarding the Greenway case. I'm afraid I forgot some important information in our talk this morning at the station."

"We'll have to do it some other time, Claire," he said. "We're exploring our most promising lead yet."

"And who may that be?" She wondered if they had already gleaned the information from Turner.

"The delivery boy. Daniel." Her heart sank a little, causing her to pull over abruptly. Luckily, there was a wide enough shoulder on the road. It was unbelievable how much time these detectives could waste.

"Why?" she said, trying to hide her inner outrage. "He's innocent. I told you that. You need to explore people who actually might be guilty."

"Danny here might be as guilty as they come. We found him lingering by Weihen's office about an hour ago. We asked him a few questions. Fortunately for us, he's a bit of a talker. But why am I telling you this? Didn't I order you to stop your amateur investigation?"

"Yes, and I have. But I have more information pertaining to Leiman Turner."

"Well, we've already been there, Clara. The man sounded convincing; he hadn't any idea about the whole case. He said he's not even near where the cifonide is produced at the plant. We think that avenue is closed."

Idiots! Turner was the supplier. Weihen was the killer. That was what she was going with at this point. Unless Turner lied. Unless he never gave the cifonide to Weihen and sprung to action himself by murdering Greenway. Either way, he was an integral part. The cops needed to stop playing around with Danny. Waste of time.

"Are you listening to me?" She was very close to yelling. Her voice was definitely raised. "I have more *information* for you. The Turner avenue is most certainly not resolved. How long could you have spoken to him anyway? I was just with you this morning. And now I need to speak with you again, understand? Now stop torturing innocent people and do your damn job." Her "amateur" investigation was back on.

"Go ahead, then. Speak."

"I want you in person. Are you at Weihen's office?"

"Get here as fast as you can," he said. The dial tone followed.

She raced to the office as fast as she could. She got there in about seven minutes flat—an incredible feat coming from the police station. As she pulled in, she saw one cop car and a delivery van. No sign of Victor's car. She noticed they wouldn't have been able to get into the office, so she swiveled her head around as she put the gearshift into park and released her seatbelt.

At the other end of the lot, she saw the backs of the two detectives standing in front of a sitting Danny. Pearson and his partner turned around as she started walking intently towards them.

"Thank you, Mr. Daniel Pincer. That is all we need from you. You've been most helpful." Pearson sped up his words as Clara walked closer. "Now that I have your information, we might be in contact."

"Detective Pearson." Clara nodded to him. "Suds." She turned her head and did the same.

"Hello, Clara," Pearson said. Remarkable that he said her name correctly. "Suds was just walking Daniel here back to his van."

Danny stood up with a smile on his face. He looked like he was a natural at talking to the police. He gave her a slight wave as he passed her by.

"Sit, Clara." Pearson sat as well. He turned to the next page of his messy pad. The page before had illegible words scrawled over it. "We think we have our jackpot with Daniel. Need more evidence, though. DNA, records, something."

"You think he's your guy? Why?" Clara asked.

"He started the delivery gig a month ago. Ex-convict. He spent three years in the slammer for providing a number of illegal weapons, drugs, and prescription pills to people. He has connections. Sentence ended a year and half ago. Needless to say, we have our eyes on him."

She squirmed in her seat. They learned that Danny was an ex-convict? Three years in prison. How did that not grant an arrest? Danny must be a real smooth talker.

"What did you have to tell us?" Suds had already rejoined with Pearson. They all sat in a line on the small bench.

Clara regained her composure and knew this needed to count. "Leiman Turner provided cifonide to Dr. Weihen. Or so he told me. He could be the supplier. Or worse, he could have lied and is the killer."

Their eyes looked unconvinced. "When did he tell you this?"

She swallowed. "In our interview two days ago."

"Why didn't you tell us earlier?" Suds was fiercely writing his thoughts into the pad. He sounded irritated.

"It doesn't matter now. I'm sorry. I have the audio file of his confession right here." She handed the flash drive to Pearson without any regret. The police now had a confession. Her fingers were crossed that the case would soon be finished.

Chapter Fourteen

*F*riday morning was the most relaxed Clara had been the whole week. She knew that, for at least a few hours, she could put thoughts of poison, affairs, and psychopaths out of her mind. She wore a beautiful, lacy dress in the morning and as she studied herself in the mirror, she somehow knew things would work out. Everything would work out. She felt rejuvenated, peaceful. It wouldn't be until the afternoon that her investigation would continue. She had this short time to breathe.

The body looked more alive than Clara thought it would. Nothing was moving, of course, but at a long distance away, she could understand mistaking Mitch Greenway for being asleep. Gently asleep. Her own eyes felt heavy and she smiled as her heart pumped even slower.

There were only two rows at the funeral, held at Greenway's mansion. Miles and Linda wanted it *very* small. They decided to skip the wake and just do an open-casket funeral. It was different. The only funeral that Clara had ever previously attended was her father's. His was held in a church and it was filled with family, friends, and even distant acquaintances. She almost felt bad for Mitch because of the meager attendance at his formal laying to rest.

Miles, Linda, Mitch's mother, and Linda's sister were all seated in the front row. The only remaining members in the family. Mitch was an only child and Linda's sister never married. In the second row, there was mom, Tracy, and herself with several professional acquaintances. The most notable was the Greenways' lawyer, dressed in a pinstripe suit and wearing a gold rolex—one of five that he owns. His name was Arthur Pendant and he was loaded. Not a billionaire, but loaded. Others seated included various maids and even the estate's gardeners, who were privately employed by Mitch himself. Dr. Weihen was not there—though it was hard to imagine he was invited. No other doctors were in attendance. Perhaps because of him.

The maids were more hysterical than the family. They kept shaking their heads and crying out as if God had done a terrible thing. Clara was sitting there, her mind absent from whatever flowery speech the officiant was giving. Eventually, they closed the casket and she saw her mom's eyes desperately holding in their tears. Tracy patted Miles' shoulder every few minutes, since she was conveniently seated behind the young heir.

"And now I'd like to invite the wife of the deceased to say a few words."

Linda hesitantly moved her body toward the coffin and stood awkwardly next to it. She held a single sheet of paper in her hand and Clara was disappointed. The speech would be brief. The funeral was beginning to be wrapped up. And she wasn't invited to the burial. Her time of peace was ending.

"My husband and I moved into this house about thirty years ago. It was passed down from Mitch's father, who was ready to move with his wife to a vacation home they owned. It was just after Mitchell Senior had retired. It was a moment of honor for my husband. He was ready to take over the family company." Linda wasn't reading from her page, Clara had noticed. She wasn't necessarily adhering to what she had written. A glimmer of hope shined that it would, in fact, be a long and boring speech in which she could tune out. And tune out she did.

After fifteen minutes or so, Linda finished her monologue. Filled with what Clara presumed were touching moments (she really wasn't listening) and sobs (she noticed those), the speech was over. And Miles stood up to the plate.

In a dry, confident tone, he said, "I've made many mistakes in my life. That man there," he pointed to the coffin, "he's made many mistakes too. Many people don't know that I was very close with my father. The tabloids and newspapers try to create drama—tension within our household that simply doesn't exist. Folks all but expect that I was neglected as a child. They think my dad was just too busy. But that wasn't the case—somehow, there was always enough time for me. I bonded with my dad and I've learned a lot from him over the years. Perhaps the most important—"

Clara started to yawn at that point. She wasn't complaining, of course. Again, this was her break.

"—thing I learned from him was the need to be truthful. Honesty is what gets you ahead in life. Some may say my father was brutally honest." A few giggles sputtered through the tiny audience. Clara was not part of this orchestra. She found it interesting that he mentioned honesty, especially after the affair and hearing Mitch's words in the bar. He continued, "That is why it is time for me to open everyone to a secret I've been keeping for a long time."

No, no. Please God, no.

"I've been seeing someone—"

Why here? Why would he bring this up at a funeral? Worshipping the dead is not a place to declare love. Clara saw Linda's head tilt in—she was prepared to hear the news. She would be shocked. They would all be shocked.

"She's the love of my life and my father, unfortunately, was against it. He was the reason I had to keep it a secret affair."

He was using the past tense too easily. It made him look guilty. She needed to think quickly—how could she stop him from saying the dreadful words? The police would know in an instant. Miles and Tracy would be doomed. She *honestly* wondered how he could be so naïve.

"Then perhaps you should honor your father and keep it secret!" Clara screamed. She was desperate. The outburst would buy some time. Perhaps it would actually prevent the day from unravelling.

She could see in his eyes that Miles had lost his train of thought. He was confused. Things were looking good until he tilted his head upwards and said, "Clara? What? You know the good news. I invited your family to hear this."

Clara's face blushed from defeat before she could feel the incoming bits of human flesh that felt sticky, spongy, and wrinkled. Linda had kissed her.

"So *you're* the one!" She exclaimed happily. It must have been crazy to think people would actually abide by funeral manners. "I knew something was going on. Miles kept his mouth shut. I can't believe Mitch knew this before me!"

Miles looked flustered. "No, mom. You don't understand."

"I most certainly do! I saw the engagement ring in your room a few weeks ago. You're marrying this girl!" She snuck another smooch. Everyone politely clapped and Clara waved Linda off of her.

"He's not in love with me. I don't know what's going on." She lied. She clung to the hope that it could still pass over without Tracy ever being mentioned.

"I'm in love with Tracy, mom!" Miles shouted. Clara collapsed in her seat, hand on her forehead. A headache had erupted—a sign of her defeat. This was supposed to be her break.

Tracy said, "Oh, Miles! You're absolutely perfect. I didn't know when you would let it be known." Clara could tell there was just a slight hint of worry in her voice. Tracy *had* to know the repercussions that would come about from this revelation. She got up and hugged him. Linda rushed over to take a picture of their hug and kissed Tracy this time. Dark pink lipstick stained her cheek, which caused Clara to wipe her own.

The officiant looked vexed as Linda began discussing wedding plans. "It must be booked! Do you want it small or grand? I think grand!" she squealed. Clara felt the morning cereal creep up her throat. The news was out. Miles had a secret relationship with Tracy Tulit and

Mitch Greenway did not approve. Miles certainly would have a large inheritance... Her last chance was to find that psychopath.

"Will you be taking over the company?" Linda's sister had asked. She had already gotten up to congratulate Miles.

"Absolutely. I need to fulfill what I was born to do. And now I have a partner to do it with." He kissed Tracy. "And we have already set a date, mom."

One by one, the few family members stood up to hug Miles and Tracy. Mom was crying of joy with Linda as they watched Miles take his congratulations. Tracy was by his side. The coffin looked out of place in a scene of joy. Only the officiant and Clara were separated from the clump of people gathered on the small patch of lawn. They both held their heads in their hands.

***

The drive to the office was fast and dizzy. Clara tried to drive slow, but it was hard when her mind was racing. Who would tell the media? What would the newspapers say? Surely, Victor would feel relieved when he heard the news. She didn't even think about seeing Victor at the office. She just drove.

The estate was a bit of a long drive to the office. Twenty minutes—a full fifteen minutes longer than her usual commute. She was tense and speeding through the yellow lights. Her next actions were hazy in her mind—as if when she got there, everything would be figured out. She knew that she wanted to discover who the mysterious psychopath was. And why Victor was seeing him in secret. Had he done something terrible in the past? If only she were lucky.

She had left the funeral as quickly as humanly possible. As everyone was expressing their grief and congratulations to Linda, she simply gave a nod to Miles and left. They had already received her sympathies and there was so little time. She really couldn't believe how stupid Miles Greenway could be—was he not nervous? Clara *knew* Tracy and even if part of her mind was blinded by this so called "love" trance, she was anxious in the back of her mind. The big sister had to save the day again. Clara decided that after all this was over, she really needed a vacation. The drama of the Greenways and Tulits was too much.

The office was dark when she pulled into the empty lot. She swore to herself as she prayed she had her keys in her purse. Why the hell wasn't Victor there? Where was he? This was not the time to make amends with the wife. Really not the time.

After shuffling around in her purse for about ten seconds, she became impatient and just dumped the whole thing in the passenger seat. The keys landed right on top. She laughed at how the circumstances always seemed to turn out the worst for her. But she calmed down because there was no gun to her head. No hurry. All she needed to do was focus.

Opening the office door, there was a rush of heat. She must have still forgotten to turn it off. She removed her shawl, switched the air conditioning on, and plopped into her desk. What was she even going to do?

She asked herself, hoping that something would magically appear.

It was against the contract she signed with Weihen to read the files of patients. She was only supposed to handle and sort them. If she broke the contract, he would have to tell all patients their confidentiality was breached and she would lose her job. She didn't know if that was the usual system in a medical office, but Victor abided by it as if it was his calling from God.

Without hesitation, she broke the rules for the freedom of the innocent and began her work. There were hundreds of files—if she were to guess, she would say maybe eight hundred. They were all the patients that Dr. Weihen had ever attended to since opening his office twenty years ago. Many left, some still came to see him.

The first file was for a man named Brody Aaron. He was seen for two months in the year 2001 for acute depression. He terminated his patient status because he was moving to New York. He had not been seen again, as marked by the signature red stamp that Victor liked to use when he had not seen a patient for a year since the last visit. Clara let out a sigh and took the next file. She knew it would be a long day. If only Weihen were here, she could weasel the information out of him. Then, she pictured him making love to his wife and gagged.

The next few hours were tedious and boring, but she had to review every file. As she came near the four hundred mark, she had found nothing even remotely suspicious, let alone any diagnoses of psychopath. Her eyes were tingling so she rubbed them and sat back in the squeaky office chair. The idea that there might not even be a file on this man worried her. If Weihen saw him in secret, why *would* there be a file? It would only be a piece of evidence.

She remained optimistic. It could have been a past patient, put into the system, and then seen *privately* years later... maybe after an accident or a crime. Perhaps a murder.

The phone rang and she nearly jumped out of her seat. It rang again and she stared at it, dumbfounded. Whoever the hell had the nerve to call the office after canceling their appointments indefinitely was not going to hear the end of it from her. But as her hand reached for the handle, she had the faint idea that a psychopath was on the other end. What if he didn't know where Victor was either?

"Dr. Weihen's office. How may I help you?" She was trying to so hard to be casual, her face was turning red. It is difficult to disguise thoughts and emotions. She still had trouble.

"Clara! You're at the office? You left so quickly I couldn't even talk to you. Isn't it wonderful? Miles' announcement? Tell me you're excited. I mean, you knew. But you didn't know at the same time. Now it's public! I will be a Greenway! Well, say something Clara!" Tracy wasn't giving her time to even say anything.

And there was no time to deal with this, but she had to tell her sister. Clara said, "I'm glad you're excited, Tracy, but that announcement caused far too many problems. People will find out that Mitch was against it— Miles said it in his little speech. You will soon be carefully watched by the police. Things do not look good for you or your future husband. You need to see that."

There was a pause. "Clara, you're always a downer. Can I just have this one thing? I'm being *married*. Mom is happy, why can't you be? Miles and I are fine—we didn't do anything. How could we be convicted for a crime we didn't commit?"

If only she truly understood the American justice system.

"Tracy, they just want to convict *someone*. If someone is held responsible, then the police will look like they are doing their jobs. This is a big case—many people are watching. If Pearson doesn't come through, the Houston Police department will take a big hit. This stuff *has* to be in those novels you read. The innocent unjustly proven guilty?"

Her voice turned into a fit of anger. "Yes, I understand Clara. Sure, we could be brought into jail tomorrow. But that doesn't stop our love! Could you at least pull one ounce of a congratulation out of your ass so I can feel like you actually care about my life?"

She didn't understand anything. She never understood anything. Of course Clara cared for her life—she was trying to save it! From the brutality of prison. The shame of having committed a murder. The police are wolves and they will eat her if she's not smart; if she doesn't understand.

"Congratulations, Tracy," Clara said, forcedly. Congratulations that your life is collapsing like a dog ready for a nap and you do not even see it, she thought. Clara hung up the phone as her sister gave a small thank you.

It wasn't the end of their conversation—she was still upset. But for now, that psychopath was still a priority.

After one more hour of searching, Clara was beat and found her mind running in circles thinking of other options. Weihen. Turner. They were all part of something, and the psychopath had to be involved. She pushed forward, and the next file was finally of considerable interest.

The manila folder was slightly bent and she immediately knew she never handled it. It was intriguing—she had handled nearly all of them, even the older ones. When she started at the office, she went over all the files and color coded them based on the times patients were first and last seen. The ones that continued to be seen by Dr. Weihen had a green sticker on the bottom, to note that they were still relevant.

There were no stickers on this file. Thus, she did not place it there. Where did it come from? She opened it and discovered it was a relatively new patient. The file simply said the patient was under the vigil of Dr. Weihen since last year. He must have been seeing him for less than a year, she thought. There were no times or dates of visits—no evidence of any visits at all. No picture, either. There were only three pieces of information on a single sheet of paper that hid within the file. The name was Trey Rasce. Blue eyes. Diagnosis: psychopath.

Scrawled in Dr. Weihen's handwriting was a single, double-underlined word. "Dangerous."

Chapter Fifteen

*C*lara rarely ever remembered her dreams, and she never before had nightmares, but the one she had that night was too bizarre to forget. The vague pictures flashed before her for a long time. The distinct sound of an organ; she was at a wedding. The first image was Miles and Tracy, laughing together. But it wasn't their wedding. Her head turned slowly around to see that Mitch Greenway and her mom were walking down the aisle. Mom was smiling, Greenway looked sinister. The music turned wicked.

A loud screech, as if the organ was breaking, could be heard. Clara turned her head again and noticed the entire church was a deep red. A rusty red that looked like it could cut you if your hand came too close. Mitch and mom walked past and when Clara saw their backs, her brain hurt and her jaw dropped. Greenway had a dagger behind his back—he was intent on hurting someone. Clara screamed but no one in the room could hear her. The dagger grew longer and more jagged as she shouted louder and louder. She was suffocating in sound. Organ music, screaming, shouts of joy, and clapping.

There was finally a second cry that everyone seemed to have heard. Clara stood on her toes to see over the crowd and saw that Mitch Greenway had collapsed on the floor, the dagger in his neck. Her mother's hands covered her face as tears streamed down her cheeks and her bridal gown looked like a sick form of Santa Claus' coat. White and red. The church bells rang and everything slowed. Then the blurry form of Clara's bedroom came into focus as she awoke.

People often said that dreams were warnings. Clara couldn't tell what this dream was warning her. She already knew why there was a dagger; it was merely a substitution for poison. And she knew Mitch Greenway was dead. She rubbed her head and stared at the wall in confusion. She wasn't anxious or scared, and there was no puddle of sweat beneath her. She was actually comfortably cool. Just curious.

She wrote down what she could recall about the dream on a lined piece of paper—the kind one would use in middle school with big spaces between the lines. As night terrors were new to her, she was inclined to savor the moment. But she knew it was nothing. Dreams were merely a patchwork of unfiled memories from the day before that often did not make sense. The supernatural did not exist. There were no signs from God. It was just a few synapses in her brain that appeared quite bizarre.

The dream gave an unusual energy that motivated her to get up and go downstairs. It was early, so Tracy wouldn't be in the kitchen. She hadn't seen Tracy since the funeral or talked to her since the phone call in Victor's office. Tracy wasn't home the night before, either. Clara ended up eating dinner with mom, vaguely asking what her plans were for the future if Mitch had seen another day. She gave partial responses that sounded like a little girl reciting her favorite fairytale.

Clara picked up the Saturday morning news on the doorstep and prepared for the worst. She didn't read the front page until she was sitting comfortably at the kitchen table with a bowl of cereal. She was relieved when she finally slipped the paper out of its cheap, thin plastic sleeve. "LEIMAN TURNER ARRESTED IN GREENWAY CASE."

Her head throbbed as she made sense of the good news. If the police were going that route, Victor would certainly be arrested in the next couple of days, if not hours. Had Pearson and Suds, or the media, missed the big wedding reveal? She hoped they had concluded there wasn't enough evidence against Miles and her sister. That would be key.

Alas, as her hope flickered, everything was revealed in the actual article. Sources said that Turner denied murdering Greenway—obviously. He also blamed Victor Wei-hen, which was a serious mistake. Pushing the blame on other people always made suspects look more culpable. Clara smiled faintly before she saw the paragraph break. The reporting changed into a twisted kind of announcement about Miles Greenway's wedding with the unknown Tracy Tulit. A small biography of Tracy was given to let readers know the kind of girl the billionaire heir fell for. A quirky, dreamy girl with no job but a passion for mystery—how the hell did they learn this stuff? Who told them? She imagined Tracy's big mouth running and spewing out fantasy.

The article only vaguely hinted that the new marriage could be a motive, but offered no true accusations.

Clara was quite satisfied. The media, and supposedly the police, were banking on Leiman Turner and possibly Dr. Weihen once more. What happened to their supposed lead on Danny? It seemed they finally used their common sense.

The final piece of information caught her eye. It mentioned the secret psychopath that Dr. Weihen had been seeing. It simply stated that he existed, but offered no more information—not even the name. Apparently, the newspaper reached out to Victor and he offered no reply. Clara had become increasingly suspicious of this psychopath, Trey Rasce. Why was Victor protecting him if he knew his innocence would soon be tested? Why wouldn't he just come clean about the whole thing? The idea soon hit her: maybe Victor was not convinced that the psychopath committed the crime. She gulped the last bite of cereal and pointlessly asked herself the age-old question: then who *did*?

Footsteps descended the stairs. She was not ready to speak to Tracy yet, but her sister's figure appeared in the kitchen as quick as lightning.

"Hey, how are you?" she asked, perky and happy. Clara was a little displeased with her demeanor.

"Struggling to still make sense of this case, Tracy. We're so lucky that the front page is about Leiman Turner, not you. It seems that's the avenue the police want to take and so be it," Clara said. She slapped the newspaper down on the table to emphasize the cover.

"That's great, Clara." She was starting up the small Mr. Coffee they kept in the corner of the counter. Clara never saw her get up this early or drink coffee.

"What's going on with you? What's all this getting up early and making coffee?" Clara asked lightheartedly. Tracy knew she was serious. Her eyes gave it away.

"It's the feeling of being engaged, Clara. You wouldn't know. It's just... so... invigorating." She smiled and turned to the coffee maker that was now squealing.

"I am happy for you, Tracy. What more do I need to say?" Clara sounded frustrated at that point. Tracy was clearly always going to be angry with her.

"I know, Clara. And it seems you're in a better mood today—is it because of what Mr. Pendant—Mitch's lawyer—said yesterday?"

Clara leaned in and said, "What did he say? I must have missed it."

She hugged her mug of steaming liquid and said, "I wasn't there either, but it's in the news." She looked over at the paper. "At least online, anyways."

"What did he say?" Clara said louder. She wasn't yelling, but she wanted to know.

"Well, apparently he confessed to a little legal information. And it concerns mom."

Clara's eyes grew wide.

She continued, "Apparently, Greenway instructed Pendant to write in a section of his will that allowed his secret lover to receive a considerable amount of money after his death. Luckily, Pendant never mentioned who the secret lover was."

"So mom is going to get money? She never mentioned anything."

Tracy finished her sip of coffee quickly so she could

respond. "That's because the section was abandoned a month ago. It was never written in."

Clara asked, "Because of Pendant or Greenway?" But she already knew the answer.

"Greenway," Tracy said.

She closed her eyes as she soaked in the information. She couldn't tell Tracy everything. Not yet.

"What do you think that means?" Tracy asked soon after. Clara was distancing herself from conversation. Could Tracy tell?

"Tracy, there's a little more to Mitch and mom's relationship than meets the eye. I believe it became a little rocky. Why else would he take her out of the will?"

"What do you think happened? She was supposed to see him the night he died, remember?" Tracy asked.

"Yes, I know. It does't quite add up. But it soon will. We will figure this out."

"About that," Tracy continued. "I'm planning for my wedding now. Greenway's murder is in the past. Nothing can be done, Clara. I think it's time to abandon our investigation. Turner or Weihen will be locked up. It's practically over."

The words that came out of her mouth aggravated Clara. She really had an incredible amount of nerve.

"What are you talking about? It's *not* over, Tracy. No one has been convicted yet. It could still be you or mom! Don't you understand? This is murder we are talking about, not a traffic ticket. It can't be paid off. We can't just stop thinking about it and hope it goes away. Leiman Turner may have been arrested, but he's not the only suspect."

Tracy finished her coffee and shook her head. "Then you continue. I'll move on with my life."

Clara started to wonder why she was even fighting for her sister as she abruptly left the room. There were now three things to do. Review the stories about Pendant, analyze the footage she had of Weihen's office for clues of Trey Rasce (although she never saw him before), and find Victor. It was time to "get real" with him and straighten out the truth. It was the only way to secure the finale of this case.

The stories were everywhere—even national news. Arthur Pendant decided to open his big mouth and say Mitch Greenway had a mistress. Every reporter gave speculation, but thankfully no one came close to the truth.

Journalists were interviewing whoever they could to get one step closer in revealing the paramour. The Greenways obviously declined—Clara was sure Linda was out of her mind by now. The headlines read, "THE FALL OF THE GREENWAY EMPIRE," and, "SECRETS OF HOUSTON'S MOST POWERFUL FAMILY." She almost felt bad. She couldn't believe she was actually thinking it, but maybe it was a blessing that Miles revealed the truth of his secret lover. He and Linda could then focus on the wedding and nothing else.

It was not a blessing. Although the newspaper chose priorities, there were still more than enough stories about the heir's affairs. Reporters questioned why he was sneaking around and even asserted that, "Mitch might have been against it from the beginning." At least they were only guessing. They weren't entirely aware of everything that was said at the funeral. Hopefully the public did not believe all the "facts" displayed on websites. Clara certainly would not.

She sat back in her chair and finalized the plans. It was hard to make the decision, but Turner and Weihen had to take the blame. They needed to be the culprits. And every loose end needed to be as tight as Linda's face.

She opened the shoebox in the back of her closet and glanced at the few objects that kept her motivated at that point. The plane tickets, hotel reservations, and credit card. A much needed vacation. The plane left the next morning and she was determined to solve this case beforehand. Everyone deserves a break. Even the pathetic being that was the combination of a lousy detective, a lousy daughter, and a lousy sister.

Opening the small laptop computer she had in the bottom drawer, she logged into the portal that saved the videos from her live feed in Weihen's office. A large error message popped up saying, "Streaming device disconnected." But she was still able to access the archive footage.

Hours upon hours. She had flagged the footage that she had found interesting beforehand—visits with Greenway, Turner. She was surprised she missed the whole Whittle situation.

She didn't re-watch the painful videos, in which Greenway admitted to unspoken things. She just sped through every bit of footage in search of a face she did not know. Nothing showed up.

Who was this Trey Rasce? By the name, he sounded Italian. Could he be an illegal immigrant? Perhaps that is why Weihen won't publicly see him. Clara searched, rewatched, paused, fast forwarded until her hands were cramping and her eyes were bulging. The power in the notebook was almost drained, so she decided to finish one last job. The video of a conversation between Weihen and Leiman Turner that certainly sounded like they were planning for the "trade." Victor talked about the color green and Turner even mentioned the word, "poison." She wondered if they spoke in code just to be sure no one was listening through the door or if Weihen knew she kept a camera in his office. If he did, why would he let it continue to stream? She shook her head at the inconceivable thought.

She shut the computer and her eyes, which only caused them to burn more. She desperately wanted to search for the latest news of the Greenway investigation—she was sure there would be more articles every twenty minutes—but she refrained. All she would see was the case slipping from her hands.

She lazily trudged over to her bed, where she collapsed. She was tired and it was only the middle of the day. She could still find Weihen, she could still find the psychopath…

Her cell phone chimed and she popped up. It saved her from giving into a long nap. She had no idea why she was so tired as of late—possibly because she knew somewhere deep down that solving this case was only a dream. When an overbearing amount of work hit her, she tended to fall asleep. But didn't that happen to everyone?

The caller ID showed exactly who she wanted to talk to: Dr. Victor Weihen. It was his cell phone, so he still wasn't at the office. She slid her finger across the screen and placed the rectangular piece of metal and glass to her face.

"Hello—"

"Clara? Is that you?" His voice was quiet and nervous. The accent seemed untamed because she struggled to understand his words.

"Yes," she said. A pause.

"Listen, Clara." This is usually when he would start to yell at her. He always began with those two words when he was irate. "I've already told you to stop talking to the police. It seems you have offered more information and it is all lies. You are not protecting me anymore, Clara. Actually, quite the opposite. You are not a detective. Just—just stay out of it!"

"Victor, where are you? Why are you speaking so quietly? I came into the office yesterday and you weren't there. There is vital information I need from you and I don't care if you don't want to provide it. You *have* to."

"Clara, listen to my words. Stay. Out. Of. It. I am at my house… but my wife does not know. I'm in the basement and I have to be as quiet as I can," he said.

It was incomprehensible why he was *trying* to make himself look suspicious. "Victor, what are you doing at your house? Your wife will find you. You're just making yourself look more suspicious. If you have nothing to hide, then why are you physically hiding?"

Another pause. He breathed into the receiver as he thought. She knew she would never get what she wanted over the phone. They needed to set up a time to meet.

He said, "I don't know why, Clara. I can't stand those detectives—Pearson and the other one with the stupid name. Perhaps that's why. Maybe I don't want to be bombarded with requests for comment by every news outlet in Houston. Even the national ones are out for information. Do not let them get to you, Clara."

"What do you mean? Why would they talk to me?"

"I don't know—I don't know—"

She slowly said, "You mentioned my name, didn't you?"

"I might have, and they might try to ask you questions. It all happened so quickly, Clara, don't you understand? You were a witness too. I had to give them something else—they were practically attacking me!" He didn't care in the least, thought Clara. He wanted to focus on the reason why he called her. He wanted to know what else she had been saying to the police. Well, she wanted to know who the psychopath was.

"Fine. I won't talk to them. But I *have* been speaking to the police. And I won't stop."

He let out a small, uncontrolled gasp. "Who? Pearson? Stop talking to him. You're only making it worse. I need to know everything you told them from the very beginning. And I want you to admit *how* you know these things. They arrested Leiman Turner for securing this poison—cifonide or whatever the hell it is. Now he's saying that he handed it off to me. A lie! That lying bastard—I should have never taken him as a patient."

Clara tried to allow as much disappointment seep into her voice as she could. "Really, Victor? You're going to contend that you have nothing to do with that poison?" She needed to aggravate him so he would divulge, but she was being stupid. She couldn't do it then. It had to be in person where she could be wearing a recording device.

"How dare you, Clara! You know I have nothing to do with that damn poison. A few days ago you were fighting for me... now you think that I did it?"

"I don't know what to think anymore, Victor. But I'm not fighting for you. I'm fighting for my family."

She could almost see the smile on his face when he said, "Ah, yes. Your family. I saw the news."

Clara ignored the comment. "We need to meet in person. At the office. I'll tell you what I told the police and you tell me everything there is to know about that psychopath that you've been seeing. I know his name is Trey Rasce. Got it? You can't hold back, Victor. There's still a chance that you can get out of all this. Just tell me everything."

An exaggerated sigh came from the other end. "Fine, Clara. At the office. Tonight. Do not let anyone know you're coming. The last thing I want is Pearson and his crew bugging the office and hearing secrets that are better left untold."

She hung up the phone and clenched her fist in victory. It was the beginning of the end.

Chapter Sixteen

As was customary in Clara's life that week, there was once again too much to be done. She had to meticulously outline every word she would to say to Victor. If she told him the honest truth about how much the police knew, he would give her the necessary information about the psychopath. If all goes well, she would send in a detailed analysis of the evidence that revealed the true killer to Pearson and Suds. That is all she could do and it was her only goal. Hopefully, they would believe the findings. If not, she can say she tried and would be on a flight the next day to southern France. Her own little vacation. No murders, no suspects or investigations, and no people to question or protect.

She dressed herself in casual attire and hopped in the car. There were a few errands needed to be done and she wanted to take her mind off of the excitement that would happen later; the final interview in the final hour. All the pieces of the puzzle would come together. Psychopath, Turner, or Weihen, someone was going to pay the price for murder.

She stopped at the Target by the galleria and picked up a small, crappy suitcase. She figured if she was going to spend the night writing a report for Pearson, she would need to have everything already packed for the trip. The bag was very much carry-on sized, but she didn't care. It wouldn't hurt to travel with a light load.

Next, she went into the mall to search for a wedding gift. She knew Tracy would be hitched before she returned, according to the dates of the plane tickets. The getaway would only last two weeks, but anything would be enough for her. This vacation was an absolute necessity, she thought.

She only gave herself an hour to roam the expensive stores with fancy window displays. She used to love shopping—watches, handbags, sunglasses. For some reason, she felt the need to have a new item every week. She was very stylish in high school; her yearbook superlative said she was most likely to be a designer. Of course, she was never interested in making any of the clothes, she just wanted to buy them.

As she looked at the absurdly overpriced pieces of material, she suddenly loathed it all. There were so many other worries in the world. Why did people care about having hundreds of pairs of shoes? They should be worried about death. Death by poison. It could clearly happen to anyone at anytime. Of all the motives, of all the suspects, she astonishingly did not see one that was worth taking a man's life. Mitch Greenway's life. She hoped there would be new details or circumstances that actually made it understandable. Indeed, people should be worried about pointlessly dying.

Clothes were not something to get Tracy because they wouldn't benefit Miles, too. Then again, why was

Clara even buying a gift? Miles could afford anything he and Tracy wanted. It could easily be something small. Not a housewares item, though, because they were presumably going to move into Miles' mansion and he already had all that stuff.

It was ten minutes before she had to start driving home to prepare for the night and following day. She passed by Brookstone and saw an eighty dollar towel warmer. She bought it, lugged it through the endless walkway of the mall, and threw it in the back of her car. It was still hot outside and she wanted it to be cold again; the coolness from earlier in the week felt good. She wiped the sweat off the back of her neck and returned to the chilly, chemically-altered draft of the car's air conditioning.

Returning home, Clara found her mother in the living room mindlessly watching one of those home-buying shows.

"Hey," Clara said. "Want to give me a hand?" She was tired of carrying the towel warmer up the stoop and did not have the energy to bring it upstairs. But she didn't know if Tracy was in the house or not, so she had to conceal it.

"What the hell is that?" mom said. Clara didn't quite care for the attitude.

"It's a wedding gift…" She lowered her voice every so slightly, "for Tracy and Miles."

"A towel warmer?" There was a short silence. Clara was ready to hear the scolding remarks about getting a towel warmer for a couple's wedding. Her sister's wedding. "That's genius."

Clara smiled. "I know, right? They already have everything they could want, but I bet they don't have this."

"Why did you buy it so soon? The wedding isn't for two weeks, Clara."

Clara fidgeted and her smile went away. She had to say that she was going on her mom's love-trip as a vacation. But she couldn't. Yet. "Oh, well, you know... I just saw it in the window and thought it would be perfect. Might as well get it sooner than later... Now help me with this thing?"

Clara's mom averted her glance back to the TV where a voice-over was asking, "Will Brad and Morgan take the home of their dreams or settle? Stay tuned to find out." A vacuum commercial began playing.

She ran over and grabbed the whole box from Clara. She rushed it up into her room as Clara brought her empty suitcase in as well. That was a mistake.

"Why did you buy a suitcase?" mom asked. Clara shuffled around her room as if she didn't know her mom said anything. She really did not know how she would take it. A vacation was necessary, she thought. Was she justified in having one?

"Where are you going, Clara?" she said seriously. It was time to lie. Clara would say she was going on vacation, but she wouldn't tell her that she kept the tickets.

"I'm taking a vacation, mom," Clara said dramatically as she put the suitcase on the bed. "I think I will solve this crime tonight and so I am leaving tomorrow. I need a break from everything. There are too many people in my life. Even if I do make a case to condemn a certain person, how do I even know that person truly committed the crime? My one goal is to make sure you and Tracy are safe. Tonight, I think you will be. Tomorrow, I'm taking a vacation. Okay?"

Her mom gave her a look as if she didn't *know* things were so stressful. As if learning mom was having an affair with the richest person in Houston a few months ago wasn't a big deal. As if finding out her sister was secretly going to marry the richest person in Houston's son wasn't worthy of concern. And as if discovering the richest person in Houston died an hour after she saw him perfectly healthy did not mess with her brain.

"Okay, Clara. Do what you need to do. But no one *asked* you to solve the case on your own. None of your family members committed a crime. The detectives should know that."

"But they don't," Clara said with her voice rising. "No one seems to understand. You need to control the world or the world will control you. If I didn't feed Pearson and Suds information, they would be after you like hawks. They would be after Tracy. And Miles. The whole family would fall apart."

"Relax, honey. Take your vacation," she said. Clara was panting. "Just be back for the wedding. You can't miss your sister's wedding." She gulped the guilt that oozed onto her tongue.

"When is the wedding?" Clara asked.

"Next Thursday. They really want to get married. It's a small event. Just family. They just want it over. Tracy just wants to be a married woman, God bless her." Her mom vaguely looked up and her eyes watered. Clara just stared at her.

In the highest voice Clara could give, she said, "I'll be there. Now let me pack and wrap this gift."

Mom started toward the door and turned around. She said, "Clara, don't worry. The world is not against you. The innocent will always remain innocent." Clara accepted her words and she left.

Clara retrieved the wrapping paper and cut it with precision, tying a nice bow around the box. She needed to find Tracy and give it to her before she left, as she would not make the wedding. Finally, she threw all of her favorite clothes in the small suitcase. Looking around the room once more, she concluded there was nothing else to pack. Nothing of importance.

* * *

Taking all the necessaries with her, Clara once again found herself in the car driving through the strange trees. It was dark outside and the plants looked like black figures against a dark blue, purple background. They were ominous and she could feel her heart beating, albeit at a slow pace. Weihen texted in the afternoon to meet at 10:00 pm. Most of the lights from the houses were turned off as she rounded the corner, heading toward Bissonnet Street. She would be at the office in four minutes.

It was uncertain how much Weihen knew. Was he aware of the camera? Did he know that she knew about Greenway's affair before the media publicized it? The questions repeated in her mind and she prepared for every outcome. She took comfort in that there was information he sought from her. There were details he did not know. She was willing to provide.

All she told the police was that Leiman Turner provided the chemical. The poison. She had recorded evidence that he admitted to taking it and handing it off to Victor. That would be a hard blow to him, for sure. He wasn't dangerous, though. He would never go after her. She would tell him that she knew Whittle was blackmailing Greenway.

Clara would come clean about the surveillance—it was to protect her mother. The secret lover of Mitch Greenway (*that* he knew from Mitch's appointments). It was only to see what Mitch thought of her—clearly she needed to know. And she expected Victor to then look at her with guilty eyes and she would give him no mercy. She would tell him that she knew everything. It was all figured out. Turner's aid, Weihen's plans, and Greenway's call for help. Now, it was time for him to tell her. To answer for his mistakes and give her the truth of the psychopath. Trey Rasce. Only then would she be able to determine who would be deemed guilty in this case. If he does not reveal the mysterious man, she would have no choice but to present the entire situation to Pearson and Suds, leaving Weihen a guilty man. A convict. He would be arrested and everyone would hail her cleverness and ingenuity. There was just one issue she needed to work out...

In the short minutes she had before the confrontation, she thought about Tracy. She thought about mom. They were bad people for lying, but they would be saved from a horrendous future. After all, she knew deep down that they couldn't have done it. They were too thoughtless, frivolous, or naïve. She could see through them and read every thought that popped into their minds. If they had committed a large crime, they would have collapsed. Miles might have been able to keep a straight face—he could have been Tracy's rock. But even rocks crack under pressure.

Clara pulled into the parking lot only to see Victor's car in the driveway. Light poured from the small window that coincided with his office. She walked in the dark to the entrance, fishing for the keys as a part of her normal routine. But the door was already unlocked.

She walked in and held her purse tight to her body. "Victor?" Clara said loudly. The dark waiting room looked serene and peaceful. There was no bright, obnoxious TV blaring the only tasteless programs and boring channels Weihen would pay for. The coffee machine wasn't constantly letting out its hourly beep and flashing red light. Her desk looked neat, bereft of the crappy pen that resided there for eight months.

His silhouette appeared at the doorway and light gushed into the room. Her eyes adjusted quickly and she soon saw his face. There were wrinkles on the forehead and bags above his cheeks. Messy hair and unshaved jaw. "Clara, come in. Don't be so loud," he said. His eyes were looking every way possible.

She walked in and he shut the door. "Victor, there is no one here. Stop being paranoid."

He played with his hands as he nervously walked over to his desk chair. He carefully said, "Don't let them fool you, Clara. They are everywhere. They know everything."

She gripped her purse and sat uncomfortably in the chair facing him. "They only know everything because I told them."

"There are things you do not know, Clara..." he said with a small smile. The German accent made him sound insane. Would she be killed tonight? It was the first time the thought occurred to her. Nevertheless, she was resourceful. She had defense.

"There is very little I do not know, Victor. And you will tell me it all tonight," Clara said. She was serious. She could see him shift his body. He smiled as he studied her face.

"You really have wonderful eyes, Clara. They are piercing and enigmatic, like little cobalt stars. I could tell they are very serious. Sharp, focused."

People complimented her eyes quite a lot. "Is that so?" she said. There was some sort of unusual tension between them.

"Have you considered contacts? Your eyes are only hindered by those glasses."

What an asshole.

She retaliated, "How is your wife?"

He reclined into his seat and they silently agreed to continue with the conversation. Victor Weihen was like that—he wanted to needle people by first appearing friendly, and then biting. Clara always thought it was a psychiatrist thing.

"How should we exchange information?" she asked. She was genuinely interested. Naturally, she feared going first because she worried he wouldn't reveal anything about the psychopath. All he wanted to know is what she told the police.

"Very good question," he said. In a swift, forward motion, he stood up and reached over to her. For a moment, she thought he was going for her breasts, and she desperately tried to back the chair up and out of the way. It only leaned backward and he was able to grab her neck. Suddenly, he had the wire, battery pack, recorder, and microphone that she had been wearing under her dress.

"I think we should play by each other's rules, Clara," he said. He handled the audio recorder as if it was fine china. Then he proceeded to throw it on the ground and smash it with his foot. "Did Pearson give you this?"

"No, of course not," she said.

"I didn't think so," he said.

"I just wanted to be safe."

He laughed and sat back in his chair. He sounded crazier by the second. Was it a full moon? Were the fluids in his brain out of place every so slightly?

"*Safe*," he said in a mocking tone. Another giggle came out of his cackling, sinister mouth. "You wanted to be safe. You just wanted to keep your family safe." He emphasized *safe* so much, he was nearly yelling. "You videotaped my private sessions to be SAFE!" He threw papers off of his desk in anger. Clara clutched her purse, but he calmed down. "Tell me, Clara. Why do you feel the need to be safe? Do you think I'm... dangerous?"

He was giving off his usual psychiatrist tone, but with rage. She didn't know how to respond; of course she thought he was dangerous. He sounded like a nutcase. And he knew about the camera.

"No, of course not, Victor," Clara said. She tried to stay on target. "Listen, do you want me to just go first? I'll tell you what the police know." Her eyes were wide. He was still looking at them. He blinked several times.

"Tell me," he said. He leaned back in his chair, signaling he wasn't a threat anymore.

"Okay. I met Leiman Turner at a Starbucks a few days ago. He admitted that he stole some of this cifonide because you asked him to. The video recordings that you seem to have found out about confirm that you most likely paid him for it. The police are convinced he's the supplier and so am I."

He didn't answer. He was just listening.

"I know you gave Greenway a sample of pills after you met with Turner. The police know that too, but not from me. They were on the body. I threw out the camera that morning so there's no evidence Turner gave you them." She paused. He waited.

"I didn't know anything about Whittle until I saw her a few days ago as well. She mentioned she was blackmailing Greenway, but she thought I knew about it for some reason. I must have missed that whole thing in my tapes. Did you know?" she asked, but she knew the answer.

"Of course I knew," he said. "I didn't know what to do—she had information. It was Mitch's problem. Not mine. I was just going to be paid and that would be that."

"Paid by who? Greenway?" He was slipping and she was stalling. She foresaw everything coming and for the first time, she actually felt the faint feeling of hopelessness. Heart racing and palms sweating, she must have been experiencing a small amount of anxiety.

He laughed. "Clara, come on. You know the answer. Don't think I'm supposed to believe that you missed it in your tapes."

Clara tried to change the topic. Her fears were growing. "Who is the psychopath, Victor? Who is Trey Rasce? Tell me. This can all go away."

Displaying his signature grin, he closed his hands together. The fingers effortlessly weaved between each other. She saw everything tumbling, about to plummet and crash. She had her back-up plan, but she didn't think she would ever have to use it. Her hand fell into her purse.

"Clara, Trey Rasce doesn't exist. You know that." He took a large breath, leaned forward, and said, "*You're* the psychopath."

The gun felt powerful as Clara pointed it steadily at Victor's chest.

Chapter Seventeen

Weihen slowly reclined into his chair. His hands were shaking as they were lackadaisically rising in the air; the dry, ripped palms faced her. She raised her eyebrows and he flinched. He genuinely had no idea the danger he was entering.

"So," she said. "You have it all figured out, don't you?" It sounded villainous, but she was never the bad guy. She just happened to have done a few bad things.

"Clara, what… I didn't mean…"

She preyed on his weakness to communicate. "What didn't you mean? I know exactly what you're suggesting. *I'm* the psychopath. The *murderous* psychopath, isn't that it?"

He looked at her with pleading eyes and she wondered if he was bluffing. There was too much malevolence in him to request mercy.

"Say it!" She said. "Say what you think I did!" She was yelling, but holding the gun steady. It was fully loaded and she had excellent aim. It was almost impossible to hold in her laughter because the whole situation was ridiculous. He looked horrified at the cackling.

Then, his face lost its resemblance to a scared animal. That sinister smile returned and Clara could tell that somewhere in his brain, he had given up. "I'll tell you exactly what you did. You sinned, Clara. You murdered Mitch Greenway. I know you did it."

"And how do you know, exactly?" she said lightly. She was perusing her fingernails so he would understand that she didn't *really* care of any knowledge that he possessed. "Why do you think I'm a psychopath?"

"Everything about you screams it," he said. "Your heartless manner, your terrible moral compass, your inability to express empathy—the list goes on. Even your eyes tell me. The eyes of a psychopath are alarming and off-putting because they seldom blink, a sign of a low heart rate. A low resting heart rate means you don't exhibit much anxiety. Yes, Clara, I knew you were a psychopath and I've been keeping a record since last month. You are my secret patient."

"You're insane," Clara said. "I'm not a psychopath, just a protector. Who the hell is Trey Rasce? A stupid ass name, if you ask me." Her words indicated humor, but her eyes indicated murder.

"It's simply an anagram of 'secretary.' Nothing imaginative, Clara. I'm surprised you didn't figure it out," he said. He was quite comfortable with a gun pointed at him. She needed to act quickly.

It was all over. Clara never planned on killing Weihen, but she had to. It was the only way—he knew everything. The only one who knew. He was dangerous; there was no way she could shut him up without using lethal force.

She adjusted the plan in her head. She would take that plane trip the next day, but never come back. Just send a letter to Pearson and that would be that. She would never see her family again, but could at least feel satisfied in her attempt to save them.

"I'm going to kill you, Victor," she said dramatically. She cocked the gun and was ready to press the trigger.

"Wait," he said. "Tell me how you did it. How did you make Greenway take the pills?"

Clara laughed at his stupidity. "You want to know, Victor?" she said, slowly, as if *she* was now the one talking to a child. But what the hell. Might have as well given him a few more minutes of life to tell her story. It would have felt good to get everything out, anyway.

"You have some nerve. Let me tell you *my* point of view and perhaps you'll understand why I have to kill you. Maybe you'll learn why you're going to hell today. It began in October when I first learned of my mother and Greenway's affair. It was at one of our family dinners. I was not too happy—I knew from the start Greenway would never leave Linda for my mom, but my mother is so delusional she doesn't get those types of things. I decided to leave it alone on one condition. I would track Mitch's true feelings by spying on his sessions with you. People tell their deepest secrets to psychiatrists, so I felt the situation was perfect. Would a tiny little camera hurt? No, of course not.

"Fast forward to December fifteenth. It was the first time I had followed Greenway and my mom on one of their dates. I was incredibly interested, you see. Where did they go? Fancy dinners or sketchy bars? Talking or kissing? Were they sleeping together? I didn't know, but I needed to. It was the only way I could fully understand their new and complicated relationship. I was sitting in the booth next to them in this absolute shit hole of a bar. That's right—Mitch treated my mother like a common whore. That was strike one. My mother, as wonderful as she is, doesn't quite see the world like we do. She lives in a limbo between reality and fiction. She had Mitch as a secret partner, but she wanted more. She wanted him to ditch Linda so they could marry and travel the world. These were all feelings left over from college, where she met him. Naturally, she didn't realize that a billionaire, who was constantly in the news, couldn't quite divorce his wife for a mistress. It would look bad for his family, his heir, and more importantly, the company.

"So my mother went off on a tangent about getting away. She gave him some kind of pathetic ultimatum and he agreed to it, the coward that he is. But you know about that, don't you? Yes, my mother even planned the trip. They would go for two weeks in disguise. It was fantasy, but Mitch played along. He bought tickets, made IDs, and setup a credit card account under false names. But my mother doesn't have common sense. If Mitch just up and left, wouldn't Linda be a little worried? Well, let's just say the specifics weren't quite worked out. At least by my mother. Because Mitch had quite a little plan of his own.

"Despite all of the glaring warnings, the first hint of danger that hit me was that night at that nasty bar. I only had one whiskey myself, so I remember it exactly as it happened. Crystal clear. My mother left to go to the ladies room, most likely to prepare for the sex they would have later in that very bathroom. So it was me in one booth and Greenway in the other. I figured he would be silent, but he made a phone call. I didn't know who he was talking to because he mentioned no name. He didn't even greet this person. He dialed the goddam phone and said, 'We have a problem. The woman I told you about thinks its serious. She wants to go away. I'll handle it, but I'll need some help.' It was quick; only four sentences. I wrote them down immediately and studied them. Who could he be talking to? What was he going to do? Well, I was lucky I installed that camera, wasn't I?

"And what I found made me furious. A week later, Greenway had an appointment with you. It was the day you unusually asked me to get you take-out for lunch and I reluctantly agreed. You were just getting rid of me. I knew there was something suspicious because I heard the lock click just as I left. You and Greenway were alone to concoct your plan.

"When I watched the footage, I learned that Greenway had every intention of getting rid of my mother. He planned to murder her, the son of a bitch. And what did you do? The supposedly moral, helpful psychiatrist? You offered to help! You *bastard*! You said you knew a guy who could secure an ounce or two of poison. You said you would lace the pills with it so that Greenway could slip the toxin into anything; food, drink, it didn't matter. As long as he could easily get it into my mother. And what would you get in return, Victor? Say it!" She pointed the gun as hard as she could.

"Five million dollars," he said. He was frozen.

"That's right! Five. Million. Dollars. You were smart about it, too. Greenway couldn't just hand it to you in cash—no. You had the brilliant idea of having him put it in his will. You might have to wait twenty years to get it, but you would get it. It wasn't urgent. Greenway would die and you would still be in your late fifties. A nice retirement fund, I would say.

"So you asked Leiman Turner, the supplier, to give you a hand. I suspect that was around the time you figured out I had a camera because you spoke in code to him. It was mind-numbingly easy to decipher, but you tried nevertheless. I learned that the poison you planned on giving Greenway was called cifonide.

"I had to act quickly. My plan was perfect and neither you or Greenway would ever see it coming. It was so simple at its core. I just needed to poison Greenway with his own drug and it could entirely be blamed on you. I had a friend back in high school who was less-than-admirable, let's just say. He had some shady connections and he had recently just gotten out of jail. He had an excellent reputation for getting things, if you know what I mean. So I told him I would pay him well if he got a job as a delivery man. He said he needed a steady income after prison, anyway. He couldn't do any more 'freelancing,' as he called it. His name is Daniel Pincer and he secured a nice amount of cifonide for me, and then delivered it right to this office. Isn't that great? Greenway wasn't even killed by his own pills! It was *my* cifonide!

"The forceful intake was straightforward. I just thought to myself—*what did Mitch Greenway do every time he came for an appointment?* The answer came to me as I was just sitting at my desk. Every patient had to sign out from the office, and Greenway was no different. I'd seen him lick a dry pen before, so why wouldn't he do it again? When the day came that you were going to hand over the poison, I was very busy. Of course, it had to be the first day back from our little winter break. That morning, I was surprised to see you in the office. I didn't worry, though. I just stuck to the plan. I threw out the camera. Then I dipped a shitty, dried out pen in cifonide and let it sit out for an hour or so. Presto! He couldn't write with it, so he dabbed it on his tongue. I could only smile as he was marked for death. It would only be an hour. No one would ever suspect a fucking ballpoint pen!" She gave way to laughter again. Weihen was traumatized, which only made her crack up harder.

"I brought the pen home later and plopped it in the cupholder on my desk. Just because it was poisoned and killed a person didn't mean I couldn't still use it again. It was evidence and needed to be far away from the office, too. Anyway, we got the phone call from the detective and you were freaking out while I pretended to be mourning. Mitch Greenway was dead and I pretended like I was on some Godsend mission to save you from prison. Quite the opposite. I planned that at the end of my mock investigation, you would come out as the sole person who could have murdered Mitch Greenway. Why? Because you're a coward, Weihen! You didn't have to get involved in Greenway's affairs. You accepted money at the price of my mother's life, you filthy bastard."

He said nothing. She continued.

"Up to this point, everything I had done was meticulously planned to the last detail. I was ready for the whole situation to go swimmingly. And it was, for a little bit. Mom told the 'dramatic' news that she was in love with Greenway. I pretended to be worried and outraged. But it was all according to plan.

"It was not until I had to commit another murder that I was sidetracked. Mrs. Whittle, that old poor woman with OCD, smacked me in the face with the news that she knew about my mother's affair. Moreover, she was blackmailing the richest and most powerful person in Houston for her own personal gain. I must have missed it in the tapes. By killing Greenway, I spared her life once. But unfortunately, I had to get rid of her because she knew too much. I couldn't have the story of my mother's affair released to the public; the detectives would go crazy! In retrospect, I regret slipping my last drop of cifonide into one of Whittle's cucumber sandwiches because a whole lot more was revealed by the media. That damn Pendant—the lawyer—admitted Greenway had a secret lover only a day ago!

"After Whittle's murder, my sister and I interviewed Leiman Turner, which gave me confidence that I could still get away with it. He gave away everything he had done and I recorded it all. He looked shocked that the cifonide was used for murder, but what did he expect? Tracy and I eventually had to go to the police station because Whittle was sacked, but they let us out quickly. Who would think a couple of young, innocent girls would commit a murder? We certainly had no motive…

"Until shit hit the fan. That's right. My own sister told me she was seeing Miles Greenway and get this— planning to marry him! Now I was covering for my mom and sister. Thank the universe both of them were unknown to the police. But the ever-so-bright Miles had the wonderful idea of announcing his love for Tracy at Mitch's funeral. Their relationship was public and I felt doomed. I thought the media would bury them—a couple of plotters killing the old man to gain the inheritance.

"But I was fortunate. Turner was arrested and everyone knew you were going to be, as well. Even *you* knew. So you called me in a desperate attempt to find out what I said to the police and in the hopes that I would maybe confess to the murder myself, considering you believed I was a psychopath." She felt out of breath. This is where it got hazy. She needed to be clear about her intentions.

She sat back and said, "So where do we go from here, Weihen? Well, now that there's no real psychopath and my cover is blown, you got what you wanted. I will be known as the Greenway killer."

He looked at her with wide, furious eyes. His hands had relaxed into his lap by now and she was trying to anticipate what he would do next. Every move had to be played right. She needed to kill him.

"Clara, I'm sorry," he said with his eyes descending onto the floor. "I never thought something like this would get so out of hand. How was I supposed to know that Greenway was going to die?"

"You knew my mother was going to die! Is Greenway's life more important?" Clara said viciously. Her finger was pressuring the trigger. Weihen squirmed.

"No, of course not. That's not what I meant. I just… I regret being involved in the whole situation." He shook his head. "Please. Spare another's life. I won't tell a soul… I just want to be done with it."

She shook her head and grinned. "Victor. You really

need to know by now that I don't give a damn about you. You don't care for my family, you insult me, and you were the worst boss imaginable."

"I—I don't have anything else to say. I won't tell Pearson or Suds. Just please let me live. I'll be alone for the rest of my life, anyway. If you killed me, no one would even visit my grave. At least Greenway will have visitors to last a lifetime. I'll be forgotten. An evaporated drop of water." He looked sad.

His words struck a note. She spent her life worrying about her reputation—how she would be perceived after her death. She would go down in history as a serial killer, but at least she would be remembered. Weihen had nothing. A victim of yet another thoughtless crime by "the Greenway killer." Was it thoughtless? No, he needed to die. It was the only way. The second she'd leave the police would be after her and she would never take the flight to southern France. And yet, his eyes looked so sad.

"Oh grow a pair, Weihen." She slouched in the chair, relaxed. The point of the gun lowered until it was aimed at the floor.

He looked up. There was a glimmer of hope in his eyes and Clara worried that she had made a mistake. "You—you'll let me free? Clara, that is wonderful news. Wonderful, wonder—" And he jumped as fast as he could right at her. His leap went higher than she ever saw a human's—way over the desk. The dagger in his hand was aimed between her eyes.

Clara used all her weight to shift the chair over. It crashed onto the floor and she fell on her side. The gun slid a few feet away. Weihen still held the knife, which now deeply cut into the wood flooring. It was clear he wouldn't be able to budge it so he made a run for the gun, but Clara was too quick. She used all of her force to scoot forward and she grabbed the heavy chunk of metal.

It was the loudest noise she ever heard. She was shocked when it was over. Her heart was pounding and her hand was hot from the tiny explosion in the barrel. Her body flew nearly two feet backward and her head was now up against the small leather couch.

She watched as blood trickled down the side of Wei-hen's cheek. His eyes had already froze still and his mouth let out an inhuman groan. The man collapsed into a pile of flesh and bone on the carpet. A puddle of rusty red liquid grew from underneath him. Victor Wei-hen was dead and Clara needed to leave.

Chapter Eighteen

The next few hours happened in a flash. Clara knew that no one heard the gunshot—there wasn't a single soul around, so she had time. She stood up and ran her hand through her hair. Passing the wooden desk, she crept up to the body. It was clearly lifeless, but she liked to be thorough. She reached down, held his limp arm in her hand, and grasped his wrist. It felt like a squishy toy. No pulse.

She then proceeded to wipe anything she touched with a small handkerchief from her purse. There would be no fingerprints left behind. The police would inevitably know it was her, but only from her confession. She couldn't risk them finding the scene and going on a search for her before the flight left in the morning. Her first major decision after the brutal scene was if she should keep the gun. She couldn't bring it to the airport—would she have needed any kind of defense before then?

The answer was no, so she wiped the prints, disposed of the unused bullets, and left it in Weihen's floppy hand. It was clear it wasn't a suicide, but that was what all the criminals did according to the detective stories and

TV shows. Tracy would have been proud. It was the rules of murder.

Clara grabbed her purse and stood in the doorway, taking one last glance at the scene. The chair she was sitting in just ten minutes before had been knocked over and broken. The items on the desk were scattered, the small area rug was folded over, and there was a large knife stuck deep into the wood of the floor. A dead man lay in the middle of everything. His figure was accented by a background of dark red. The black gun rested in his hand. It was the final time she would ever see the office. To think that just eight months before, she actually thought she had a stable job. Hilarious.

She smoothly walked through the waiting room and out the door, locking it behind. All lights were shut off—she didn't want there to be a single indication that anyone was there. She had to play it safe. No early warnings.

She drove home like it was the end of a work day. Only this time it was late—as if she stayed to do extra hours. As if she was dedicated to her job and she now deserved to go home, have a glass of wine, and maybe soak in a bathtub of warm water and scented bath salts. She turned up the volume in the car and drowned her thoughts in the mystical, leaden sounds of talk radio. "Billy Z from 101.3" was discussing the news of the day. Apparently, the police were going to let Leiman Turner walk. It all didn't matter anymore. Though she was sure Turner would eventually be convicted for aiding a planned murder after her full disclosure.

Pulling into the driveway, she saw her house was lit up as usual. Every other house was dark, but her household never obeyed the natural laws of sleep. The Tulits were night owls and even when they gave into slumber, the lights stayed on. It drove mom crazy. Clara vaguely prepared to talk to Tracy. She had to say goodbye.

Tracy was sitting on the couch immersed in television. Clara assumed her mother was already sleeping upstairs, most likely the result of a few bottles of wine. That was the new normal.

"Hey," Clara said as she dropped her purse on the ground.

"Where were you?" Tracy asked without turning her head.

"Oh, I just went out to see a friend." She walked over and sat in the chair next to the couch.

Tracy shifted her eyes and did a double take. She sat up. "What the hell happened to you?"

Crap. Clara probably looked like crap. Combing her hair with her hand wasn't the best cover-up after a rather combative fight. "Oh, you know…" She couldn't think of anything. "It was a crazy night."

"You? A crazy night? Okay," Tracy said sarcastically. Even Clara laughed at how unbelievable it was.

"So when's the wedding?" she asked casually. She wanted to ease into breaking the news.

"Next Thursday, Clara. The planning is going so well. It's going to be gorgeous—the perfect wedding. Linda has been such a help in the whole process. I'm glad you're now okay with me marrying Miles. You really have to stop worrying—no one is going to get hurt."

"I heard they're releasing Leiman Turner soon," Clara said.

"It's all speculation—no one actually knows." She was wrong.

"Hey Tracy, I have something to tell you that's a little difficult for me to say…" She had to word it in the best possible way.

"What's that?"

"I won't be at the wedding," Clara bawled. It was her best fake cry in a while. Actual tears—that's a fact. Water was streaming down her face and it helped with Tracy's reaction.

"You're not going to be at the wedding? Wh—Why?" Her sister looked very upset. She moved closer to half-console, half-berate Clara.

"Well, I'm going away for a little while," Clara lied. It wasn't for a little while. She would never see her again.

"Where?"

"I can't tell you, Tracy. Please don't ask questions. I won't be able to answer them. I'm just taking a little vacation. Clearing my head. Weihen's closing the office, so I'm out of a job. I need a little break." She said it in a pleading manner. She hoped Tracy wouldn't be confused.

"I'm so confused, Clara," Tracy said. "Why can't you go on a vacation after the wedding?"

"I can't, Tracy. I'm sorry." Clara went over to hug her sister, who reluctantly accepted. She wiped the artificially genuine tears off her cheek and gave a *thank you for understanding* smile.

"Wait," she said excitedly. "I have something for you."

Clara ran up the stairs to retrieve the wedding gift. It was the perfect time to distract Tracy from thinking—she would certainly be putting things together in her head. After all, how sketchy was it that Clara was leaving so quickly and without warning? The towel warmer sat in her closet. It looked beautiful in its nice wrapping paper and bow. No card, but there was nothing really to say.

Clara practically tripped as she lugged it downstairs and found Tracy in the same position that she left her. She handed it over and her sister was hesitant to open it.

"Maybe I should wait for Miles," she said with a finger on her lips. Clara nearly rolled her eyes. She was leaving forever—she needed to open the stupid gift.

"No, it's fine. Open it, I'm too excited."

She agreed and tore the wrapping paper into confetti, as she always did when opening gifts. Every Christmas, mom had to vacuum for an hour because of her. It was cute, but messy.

"Thank you Clara. This is awesome." Tracy hugged her and that was the end of it. She didn't expect much; it was only a towel warmer, after all. She left her downstairs with the mess of paper and the shiny, brand new bathroom amenity. That was the last time she saw her sister.

Upstairs, Clara planned to go to her room but found herself veering in the other direction and quietly opening her mom's door. It was dark. Mom was stretched out on the bed in her day clothes. A half-empty bottle of wine was on the nightstand and she was out cold. Clara watched her chest rise and fall in sync with her gentle snoring.

Inching closer with care as not to wake her mother, Clara found herself right next to the bed. She inaudibly whispered, "Goodbye," and quitted the room.

The time had come to write her confession and she was fully prepared. It was easy to write—a hefty fifteen hundred words in about a half an hour. No editing, no polishing. Just the raw truth. It would be a bombshell. The media would go crazy the next afternoon, she thought. The psychopathic secretary that killed three people. The unfaithful, murderous billionaire, the psychiatrist that sold out for money, and the old lady that wanted to make a quick gain from the whole situation. Turner would be screwed. Clara only felt guilty about Danny—he helped her secure the cifonide and the gun. It wasn't right for her to sell him out. But she had to do it—the only way. After three murders, her mother was alive and her sister was going to marry. She never thought it would be at the sacrifice of her reputation, but her family was safe.

***

ONE MONTH LATER

Clara now resides in a tiny apartment that she paid a small sum of cash for—directly withdrawn from the account that Mitch Greenway so graciously put one hundred thousand dollars in. She has been picking up on French ever so slightly, but she is nowhere near fluent. Interestingly enough, she has come across quite a lot of people who speak English. Naturally, she left Marseilles and now resides somewhere else in the general area of southern France. She remains in the background and goes unnoticed. She blends in as just another fish in the fleet. A witness, but not a participant, of life.

Her name is now Abigail Richmond, the alias Greenway created for her mother so long ago. The fake ID has never failed and the credit card is perfect. Clara Tulit has forever left the face of the earth and she is relieved.

She has been following the events in Houston, Texas, closely from a cheap laptop she bought the day she arrived in the foreign country. The entire story unfolded and the media ate it up. Not a day goes by without a new article and it will not end for a while. As expected, Turner was arrested. They requested that her mom answer a few questions, but she declined and they backed off. The police thought that she would have an idea of where her daughter went but she insisted she did not. It is hard to tell if she figured out that Clara used her tickets or she was oblivious to the whole thing. Either way, Pearson and Suds would never find out.

As for Tracy, she presumably had a wonderful wedding. The details were scarce because it was a small, private affair, but the descriptions left Clara in awe. The color schemes of baby blue and lavender were apparently remarkable. The day she read about the wedding, she cried. It was the first time she had truly bawled in five years, since her father's funeral. The honeymoon, on an undisclosed island somewhere near the Caribbean, is still going on. Clara often wonders how much Tracy thinks of her. Mother too. Do they condemn or celebrate her? What if they didn't understand the complicated reasons why she needed to protect them? She tries to push these thoughts out of her mind, but they show up on a daily basis.

The search for Clara Tulit is still ongoing, but they have made zero convincing leads. She is confident she will never be found—if she sees any news that even hints France, she will just leave and move onto the next hiding place. She is quite comfortable with a life on the run. It's better than a life in prison… or no life at all.

Miles has taken over the Greenway Oil Company, which despite all of the headlines, has done remarkably well. Tracy and Miles will lead happy lives, Clara has no doubt. Greenway's lawyer, Arthur Pendant, retired amidst the controversy. He still did not disclose who the lover was. He never would—she made quite sure of it with a nice little threatening note. A last minute touch as she was preparing to leave the night before her flight. Mom didn't need that kind of negative publicity.

Pearson and Suds clearly received her written confession, as evidenced by the fact that she is now accepted as a serial killer. Is she truly a psychopath? She wouldn't dare see a psychiatrist to find out. It would be too risky. She left the confession in a sealed envelope on her bed just as she was leaving for the airport. It had a note attached telling either her mom or Tracy to hand it over to Pearson and Suds. The note explained the envelope as her final report, but requested that none of her family members open it. "Please allow only the police to read this," she wrote.

She has changed her appearance. Her hair is now a light blond, cut quite short. She did it herself in her bathroom in Texas. She would have made a fine hairdresser, she thought as the hair went down the drain. Pearson and Suds would look at every camera in every airport in the southern states. They wouldn't find her—a blond in loose clothing with huge sunglasses and ridiculous makeup. Abigail Richmond was truly a sight to see.

It is a mystery where to go from here, but Clara knows she will never be able to go back to the United States. She would never be able to see her family again. Tracy and mom. She feels fine now that she could see them on the news every day, but soon they would stop being of interest. They would slowly fade away. Clara Tulit often took most of the headlines—they say she was most likely insane. They say Weihen knew she was dangerous and all of her old shitty friends have come out from their dusty corners to talk about her.

"She was always a little off," one girl said. It was Suzie Kamen. Clara probably said two words to her in ninth grade, and now the girl acts like she was her best friend or something. It's sad when someone does things like that for attention. But Clara just brushes it off and closes the browser. It doesn't matter anymore. Nothing matters.

She does not regret what she did. Murder as the result of defense is not looked upon as evil, so why does everyone make it a big deal? She was acting out of defense for her mother. The woman was going to be poisoned just because she fantasized a little too much. Clara wouldn't have that. Even owners of billion-dollar companies need to learn that people deserve more. Lives were worth *more* than his reputation. She simply flipped the coin and showed that a person like Mitch Greenway is mortal. If he messes with her family, he will pay the price. And so he did.

Whittle happened to be pulled into the wrong situation at the wrong time. Her greed is what drew her in. All she wanted was money from Greenway. Clara likes to think that she saved the old lady by killing

Mitch. He would have went after her once her mom was finished off. No one blackmails a billionaire and doesn't wind up lifeless in a dumpster in the middle of nowhere. She saved her once, she killed her once. They were even.

As for Weihen, he had it long coming. A terrible employer, a terrible person, Victor Weihen was the epitome of selfishness. He hungered for money and power and left little empathy for anyone else. An offer for millions of dollars? He took it without a break of a sweat, fully aware that his actions were going to leave someone dead. He orchestrated and plotted—he would have certainly gone to jail for life. If only her real plan worked out and he was accused of the whole thing. She could still be living in Houston and he would be in state prison, locked up forever. Just thinking of him sickens her. The dead body on the floor comes to mind nearly every day. In a way, she saved him, as well. From a life of torment and imprisonment. She rescued him from paying for his inexcusable actions. And she hates herself for it.

As Clara sits on her double bed in the smallest bedroom she has ever seen, she finds relief that her story is over. It is all in the past. Perhaps in many years, when she is long gone, someone will correctly understand the actions of the "Houston billionaire murderer," or so she is called. Someone will realize it is just a tale of a woman saving a life. A familial sacrifice. *She did what she had to do.* All she wants is someone to realize that she was not in the wrong and she'd be happy.

Now that the miserable days have ended, she no longer thinks about death. The idea that her mother would have been gone kept her up at night for a while, but she now sleeps soundly. She used to worry that when she died, she would be forgotten. It may not be the best situation, but she will certainly be remembered. She was a murderer. A liar. A psychopath. She will go down in history as one of the evil people of the world; her second death has been postponed. She is not immortal like so many, but she will be remembered. Clara Tulit will not die for a long time.

CPSIA information can be obtained at www.ICGtesting.com
Printed in the USA
BVOW02s2338210615

405041BV00001B/25/P